Murder in Knoxville

A Collection of Sam Jenkins Mysteries

Wayne Zurl

Published by
Melange Books, LLC
White Bear Lake, MN 55110
www.melange-books.com

A Murder in Knoxville ~ Copyright © 2017 by Wayne Zurl

ISBN: 978-1-68046-507-5

Cover Art by Lynsee Lauritsen

To all the people who want to read about real police work—the excitement, the boredom, the drama and the comedy.

A Labor Day Murder

Wayne Zurl

A Labor Day Murder
Wayne Zurl

I don't think she really hates me, but she does cringe every time I walk into her office. Maybe it's the lawyer jokes I tell. Or maybe it's how I show a lack of respect for the local politicians. I guess I'm comfortable with our relationship. And someday Moira may learn the Jenkins method of compromise: We talk about it and then do it my way.

"You expect me to go before a judge and ask for a warrant so you can search a restaurant for the proceeds of illegal gambling?"

"Yes, ma'am. That's why I'm here," I said.

"Lord have mercy, Sam. It's only a card game."

"In the last seven days, my cops have made two DUI arrests of men leaving that place after hours. Both people said they were playing cards, and the owner was chopping the pot."

"If you held a card game at your home wouldn't you accept some reimbursement for the food and drink you offered the players?"

"This guy is taking fifteen percent from each pot. They're playing dollar-five poker. That's more than the goombahs get back where I used to work. He's also operating a cash bar, serving untaxed moonshine. His restaurant only has a beer license."

"I hear what you're sayin', Sam. I understand. Do you understand that Audie Blevins has operated that restaurant for almost forty years? His daddy owned it for Lord knows how many years before that. Audie's brother is the chairman of the county commission, and Audie's a very, and I emphasize very, big supporter of and contributor to the local Republican party."

"Well, three cheers for Audie. He sounds like a real good ol' boy. Do I have to tell you I don't give a rat's ass to whom he's related or to

1

what he contributes?" I asked.

Moira Menzies is a pretty blonde, around fifty, and if she smiled more often would be even more attractive. She's also the chief assistant district attorney general for Blount County, Tennessee. Whenever I need a search or arrest warrant, I deal directly with her.

For a moment before she spoke, she closed her eyes and shook her head. "You're not goin' away, are you?"

I smiled at her. My lady-killer smile has been known to melt the coldest heart.

"Nope."

We were sitting in her second floor corner office in the Justice Center, overlooking the new jail.

She stood up and put her hands on her hips. "Don't try that smile on me, Jenkins. More cops have tried that act than I can count."

I looked up at her. "Yeah, but I'm the only ex-New York cop you know, and I'll bet I'm the best lookin' police chief in the county."

She dropped the pencil she'd been holding onto her desktop—with a little more force than necessary. "You sure ain't the most modest. Come on, I'll walk you up to the judge's chambers."

Twenty minutes later, I had my 'no knock' search warrant for the Iron Skillet restaurant.

"You think the judge will drop a dime on Audie and give him a heads-up about the warrant?" I asked.

"Judge Myers is a pretty straight shooter, but anything's possible. Audie *is* well-connected."

"Let's hope Judge Myers believes in truth, justice and the American way."

"Let's hope he believes in at least the first two," she said.

* * * *

At 11:30 Saturday night, six of the twelve cops employed by Prospect PD and I waited outside the Iron Skillet on Sevierville Road. Five of us had driven our personally-owned pickup trucks to haul away the furniture, file cabinets and other accouterments used by the owner to promote gambling and sell untaxed alcoholic beverages.

"Twelve cars plus Audie's. Must be a couple of games goin' on,"

Sergeant Stan Rose observed.

"I guess," I said. "No one new has shown up for thirty minutes. Time to kick in the door."

Stanley nodded. "Sounds like a plan."

"I wish we had a paddy wagon. It looks unprofessional using our own pickup trucks."

"A paddy wagon? Sometimes we look like the Keystone Cops, but there's no reason we need a paddy wagon."

"Each precinct had a paddy wagon in New York."

"You own a pick-up in New York?"

"Of course not."

"Well?"

"You sayin' I'm getting like the locals?"

"I've got no theory. I'm just presenting the evidence."

"Don't you feel stereotypical driving a Cadillac?" I asked.

Stan is from Los Angeles and usually sounds like a Cal Tech graduate. "I do not. A brother's got to look good when he's on the road. Clean car, pretty woman…you unnerstand what I'm sayin'?" Occasionally he lapses into Ebonics for my benefit.

"Uh-huh. My man. Right on. What it is!" I said, sounding more like a Black Panther than a police chief.

"Honky racist."

"You wish."

"We ready to go?" he asked.

"I was ready before you started all this ethnic crap."

"Well then, great white leader?"

"My wife doesn't give me as much trouble as you."

Stanley gave me a big grin. "Come on, man. It's show time."

I keyed the portable radio I held, "Prospect-one to all units—do it."

Officers Bobby John Crockett and Vernon Hobbs pounded on the front door. Harlan Flatt, Leonard Alcock and Junior Huskey covered the back door and the windows at the rear of the restaurant. Stanley and I moseyed up to the front entrance.

A thin man with short dark hair and a wispy mustache, looking like a bartender in his white apron, answered the door. The two cops pushed their way in. Stan and I followed.

3

"Police department. We have a search warrant. Nobody move!" Bobby called out.

No one moved.

"Where's Audie Blevins?" I asked, waving a copy of the warrant in my left hand.

"That would be me," said a short, well-dressed man of about sixty.

I handed him the paper.

"This is a warrant to search your premises for evidence of illegal gambling and untaxed liquor," I said. "I see two card games. Care to explain anything?"

"Jest some friendly games, officer. We get t'gether ever once't in a while ta play cards. Nothin' more."

"Have a seat, Mr. Blevins, and don't touch anything." Turning to the bartender I said, "What's your name?"

"James Begley, sir. Most ever' one calls me Jammer."

"Okay, Jammer, you have a seat, too."

I told Bobby Crockett to open the back door and let the other three cops in. While Stan and I took names, and capped the drinks on the tables with Glad-Wrap, the boys searched the restaurant, the adjacent office and the storerooms.

The quickest way to put pressure on a restaurant owner is to threaten to take away their liquor license. I demanded a copy of his from Audie Blevins. As I recorded all that information, Junior Huskey got my attention.

"Sam, look-it here." He handed me two folders and a well-stuffed, padded manila envelope. One folder was marked *players*; the other was unmarked. The envelope was full of cash. I looked over the two-page list of players. There were over thirty names with telephone numbers. The unmarked folder had several loose-leaf pages showing dates and dollar figures. The dates went back more than two years.

"Good work, kid," I said to Junior, "a list of gamblers and profits from the games. You ought to be a detective."

"I could live with that, boss."

I gave him an encouraging thumbs-up even though we have no detectives at Prospect PD.

Crockett and Harley Flatt carried in four plastic, gallon milk jugs all full of clear liquid.

"They's about six or seven more jest like these in the back," Harley said. "Take a whiff, boss."

He popped the cap off one jug and lifted it to my nose.

"Yahoo." I took a half step backwards. "Smells like pure alcohol. Must be 190 proof or better." I turned to the closest table of players. "Any of you guys feel like you're going blind?" No one seemed to enjoy my attempt at humor. "Harley, confiscate everything and box up all these glasses we've put tops on. We'll let the Alcohol, Tobacco and Firearms people analyze this for us."

Then Vern Hobbs walked up, extended his hand and showed me a large revolver.

"Got this in the office, boss. Nice lookin' gun."

It was an old Smith and Wesson model 1917, .45 caliber revolver…a revolver that fired .45 automatic ammunition.

"This pistol have a story behind it, Mr. Blevins?" I asked.

"I got a right ta keep a gun in my restaurant. It's all bought an' paid fer, all legal-like," he said. "Ain't yew ever heard o' the Second Amendment?"

I wanted to give Audi the finger, but resisted the urge. "Bag it, and tag it, Vern. I'll send it off to be checked."

All the players we met that night were on the list Junior found. I wanted each man charged with participating in illegal gambling, privately interviewed and a statement taken from each one. We had several hours of work ahead of us.

When we finished issuing appearance tickets to the players and Jammer Begley, we took Audie Blevins to Prospect PD to process his arrest. At three in the morning, we released him on one hundred dollars bail. Two sixty-inch round tables, sixteen chairs and two tall file cabinets filled the lobby of our office and the squad room. The evidence closet held eleven-and-a-half gallons of moonshine, over three thousand dollars in cash and a few other evidentiary items taken from the Iron Skillet. In a few hours, the Sunday eight-to-four shift would arrive at work, wonder what the hell went on the night before, and then life would go on.

* * * *

At 8:50 Monday morning I walked through the back door of the PD. Sergeant Bettye Lambert sat at her desk in the front office.

"Morning, Betts," I said.

She turned and looked at me but said nothing. I thought it was time for some basic male-female interpersonal relations work.

"My goodness, Bettye, but don't you look exceptionally nice today. You do something different with your hair or—"

She cut me short.

"Don't start your charmin' act on me, Sam Jenkins. What have you done to my police station? All this junk looks like we're havin' a yard sale or somethin'."

Bettye is forty-two years old, blonde and beautiful. Perhaps the loveliest desk sergeant on the planet.

"Bettye, we did a gambling raid Saturday night. This is just a collection of what we confiscated."

"Gambling?" She tilted her head. "Well, Lord have mercy. I just hope you find a place to put all this before too long."

"Yes, ma'am, I will. Don't worry. Last thing I want to do, Sergeant Lambert, is make you angry." As I smiled at her, I wondered who the real boss was at my police department.

She shook her head. "What am I going to do with you, Sammy?"

"What?"

She frowned and shook her head again. I decided to find a storage spot for the confiscated property.

Around eleven o'clock I hopped into my gunmetal gray, unmarked Ford with Audie Blevins' Smith and Wesson revolver and headed toward Knoxville. Half an hour later, I entered the Federal building at 710 Locust Street, went into the FBI field office and found my friend, Ralph Oliveri.

"You did a gambling raid in Prospect?" He sounded surprised.

"Yes, and a good one, too. Player list, records of profit, a bag full of cash, untaxed alcohol and a handgun I need you to send off to get checked."

"It's never ending with you, isn't it?"

"Lighten up, Ralphie. If it wasn't for me, you'd have to go out and drum up your own cases."

"I hope I don't have to remind you of all the favors you owe me." Like me, Ralph is from New York. He acts like it, too.

"I have them all written down, paisan. I never forget anything."

Ralph rolled his eyes.

"Hey, it's after noon," I said. "I'll let you buy me lunch, and I'll tell you how much I appreciate your help."

He shook his head. "Amazing! Just freakin' amazing."

We ate at Chesapeake's at the intersection of Broadway and Western Avenue, and because Ralph wouldn't stop complaining, I paid for our crab cake platters and pints of Cherokee Red ale.

I didn't have great expectations of finding anything sinister, but I was anxious to get a report back after the gun was processed. But as I've learned over the years, the wheels of justice often turn slowly—especially for a small police department in East Tennessee. I resigned myself to a period of waiting.

Back at the PD, I found our lobby clear of the confiscated furniture.

"I see Mr. Files and Spurgie were as efficient as ever in cleaning up *your* police station," I said to Bettye.

"They were. Thank you very much. Now you need to call Moira Menzies at her office."

"Sure. She say what she wanted?"

"Not to me. Probably has to do with your gamblin' raid." Bettye smiled and fluttered her eyelashes, knowing how easily she can influence me with a little flirting. "Good gracious, a gamblin' raid in li'l old Prospect," she said, "You'd think this was Brooklyn."

I needed to show a little attitude. "Ey, whadda yoo know 'bout Brooklyn?" I said, sounding like I just stepped off Flatbush Avenue.

"Only what you tell me, darlin'."

"'Lady, yoo bedda tawk nice 'bout Brooklyn. Me and da Dodgers bote come from dare."

"Lord have mercy, but don't y'all talk funny."

* * * *

Moira Menzies made our phone conversation very short and simple, "Sam, I'd like you to give Audie Blevins his furniture back. We don't need it for the prosecution. You really shouldn't have taken it anyway."

Obviously, Moira was unfamiliar with Jenkins' law of criminal procedure.

"Audie is lucky I didn't find a deck of cards in the front seat of his Lincoln. I could gain a bunch of points with my friends at the FBI if I gave them a new Town Car from an asset forfeiture case."

She didn't comment on that idea.

"You also should give back the cash you confiscated. His lawyer claims that's only capital from the restaurant," she said.

"Check the inventory. The money taken from the register and the office safe could be restaurant money. We found the envelope with over eighteen hundred dollars in small bills in a locked file drawer, along with a list of players and his ledger sheets showing the proceeds of his gambling operation. Let's give back his biscuits and gravy money. Keep the eighteen large to buy new paper and pencils for the sheriff's department."

"Sometimes you're utterly impossible, Sam."

"Can a doctor cure that with medication?"

She ignored the question. "Are you opposed to a quick plea bargain?"

"Of course not. This is a gambling collar, not a murder. Give him a hefty fine. He made money on the card games. Make him lose money in the court system. He'll learn the economics of it."

"Good. His lawyer is anxious to let him plead out."

I shrugged. "By the way, Ned the Fed at ATF may want to speak with Audie after their lab analyzes the moonshine I gave them. I doubt he made it himself."

"You're a hard man, Jenkins."

I laughed.

"What?" she asked.

"No comment."

"He also asked to have his pistol back. He wants protection for his restaurant."

"If he wants protection, tell him to buy a condom. He has to wait for the FBI to finish vetting the gun. I'll send him a note when he can have it back."

"Audie Blevins is not a member of an organized crime family. Is it

8

necessary to treat him like one?"

"I treat all my customers the same. It's easy to avoid issues of constitutionality that way."

"Sam?" Moira gave an exaggerated audible sigh. "Oh, never mind. Please give the man his tables and chairs back."

"As you wish, madam."

"Oh, for the love of God…Good bye." She hung up.

Old George Files and his assistant Spurgie Dent weren't too happy when I told them about bringing the two tables and sixteen chairs back up from the basement storage room when Jammer Begley and a helper who looked a lot like a young Wallace Beery stopped by with a truck. Later that day Audie came in personally to get his night deposit bag full of restaurant cash. I let Sergeant Lambert handle that distasteful transaction.

After Audie left the building, Bettye and I and the boys of Prospect PD were once again back to business as usual—for a while anyway.

* * * *

Several days later, Ralph Oliveri asked, "Hey, can I buy the luck you always seem to have?"

"What luck? I'd prefer to think of it as superior police abilities. What are you talking about anyway?"

"The gun you gave me. Give yourself a gold star. You got a jackpot."

"Keep talking, Ralphie. I'm starting to get excited."

"The gun was used in a homicide near your neck-of-the-woods. In September of '06, a guy named Harvey-Dean Mullins was shot to death in his Maryville home. The Blount County Sheriff has the open case. Two distinct sets of prints are on the gun. One matches to your defendant. The other is an unidentified partial. The gun's on its way back to us as we speak. Pretty good stuff from your little jerk-water PD."

"I'm sending my thanks to you and all the little G-men involved. You're fine Americans."

* * * *

I walked out into the reception area to tell Bettye the good news.

"Hot damn! Am I good or what?"

"Finest detective I've ever met. Not exactly the most modest, but you do make things interestin'."

"You forgot slick as a ribbon and more dashing than Dirty Harry Callahan."

"No, I didn't forget. I just didn't want you to accuse me of sexual harassment," she said and gave me one of her big smiles.

"Someday, Sergeant, you're gonna get me into trouble."

"Promises, promises."

* * * *

I sat in my oversized swivel chair with my feet propped up on the right corner of my desk and dialed a number in Maryville, the next town to the west.

"Mr. Costello's office, may I he'p yew?"

I knew the voice.

"Hi, Stephie. How's my favorite legal secretary today?"

She must have recognized my New York accent. "Oh, hi, Mr. Jenkins. I'm jest real fine. You doin' aw rot today?"

"Fine as fur on a frog, young lady." She giggled. "Your fearless leader in the office?"

"He shore is. Yew hold on now." She connected me.

"Hey, Joe, how's it going?"

"Sam, you doin' aw right today?"

"I'm okay, but I'm going to throw a monkey wrench at you and one of your clients."

"Audie Blevins?"

"Uh-huh."

"ATF want him now for the moonshine?"

"They might, but I've got something a bit heavier. You sitting down?"

"Go ahead. I hear Mr. Blevins' checkbook opening."

"That old revolver we confiscated—the FBI says it matches bullets taken from a murder victim in Maryville last year."

"Oh, Lord have mercy. You arrest him again?"

"Called you first. I could get a warrant, but why don't you bring him into my office for a chat?"

"How's tomorrow, first thing?"

"Nine o'clock's good for me."

He sighed. "Okay, we'll see ya then."

I spent the rest of the morning getting as much background information on Audie Blevins as I could. Then I made another phone call.

"Criminal investigations, Officer Shuman. Kin I he'p ya?"

"Jackie, Sam Jenkins. How's it goin'?"

"Hey, Sam, you doin' aw rot today?"

Everyone in East Tennessee asks the same question, but nobody ever expects an answer.

"You know anything about a murder from last year? Guy named Harvey-Dean Mullins? The body was found in a house on Ellejoy Road in Maryville?"

"Sure do. Me'n Neil Brickman did the crime scene work. Doyle Snoderly now, he was the detective."

"Snoderly around?"

"Well, yes and no. He ain't around here no more, but he's around."

"Care to explain?"

"He got hisse'f the assistant chief's job over to Maryville PD." He pronounced it Murr-vull.

"That was a big career advancement."

"Y'all know how it is."

"Yeah, almost like real estate. The three most important things in Tennessee law enforcement…connections, connections, connections."

"I hear that."

"What do you suppose Doyle did to qualify for that job?"

"Huh," he snorted. "You tell me."

I didn't bother answering that rhetorical question. "Your case is still open. Know who picked it up?"

"Hang on a second." I heard him tapping keys on his computer. "Yep, Bo Stallins."

"Okay, Bo around today?"

"He's on the road. Mind tellin' me why you're askin'?"

"I found the gun that killed your victim."

"Damn! Some people got all the luck."

"Can you hook me up with Bo? I want to speak with him as soon as possible."

"Sure can. By the time you git here, I'll have him back in the office fer ya."

"Thanks, Jackie. Hey, do me a favor? Keep all this quiet until I get there. My suspect is pretty well connected himself."

"Gottcha covered, Chief. See ya later."

* * * *

"Thanks for the paperwork, Bo."

Detective Stallins was fortyish, taller than me by a couple inches, about six-two, but thinner than my hundred and eighty pounds.

"I can tell you that from what I know now and who the suspect is, the shit's gonna hit the fan on this one," I said. "You could dump it on me and save yourself some grief."

"Well, thank ya, Sam. Personally, I don't care if I do it, but if you're offerin', I shore won't say no. You need any he'p?"

"I'd like one of you," I looked from Bo to Jackie, "to run the unidentified partial print the FBI found on the gun through the local non-criminal files. I'll have that for you as soon as the gun and the reports come back. Other than that, I don't think so. But if I run into something, I'll give you a shout. Honestly, for your sake, best stay a mile away."

"I hear that. And I 'preciate it. I truly do," Bo said.

Jackie nodded in agreement. He was a young-looking thirty-five, a few pounds overweight and wearing the summer uniform of a crime scene investigator: A white polo shirt with a Blount County Sheriff's Office badge embroidered onto the left breast and a pair of black tactical pants.

"Okay, guys, I'll let you know how I make out."

* * * *

What I learned from a quick look at the case folder was that Harvey-Dean Mullins had been married to the former Dixie Blevins, Audie's daughter. *Small world, isn't it?*

My next stop took me to the sheriff's Records Bureau. I asked a clerk to pull any and all files they had on Harvey-Dean or Dixie Mullins and any of the Blevins clan. With the first two, I got a typical package, full of domestic disturbances, husband-wife fights resulting in a few arrests where the cops removed Harvey-Dean for the night, and Dixie failed to appear in court the next morning to sign the complaint. Dixie used the Blount County deputies as her personal bouncers, but failed to follow through and perhaps, keep her husband from using her as a punching bag. All that was nothing unusual until Harvey-Dean was found with four two-hundred-and-thirty grain .45 caliber slugs in his scrawny body. Finding the gun that fired those slugs ten months later in his father-in-law's restaurant certainly made things a lot more interesting, especially when the reports noted Dixie's occupation as a bookkeeper at the Iron Skillet.

From the sheriff's office, I went to Blount Memorial Hospital. After getting the same old rhetoric about the confidentiality of medical records and using my same old spiel about conducting a homicide investigation and coming back with a subpoena, the clerk relented and told me that Dixie Mullins had been a frequent visitor to the Emergency Room. Dixie claimed she was accustomed to walking into doors, falling down stairs and getting bruised up during her daily accident-prone life. Injuries like that were all signs of unspoken spousal abuse even a rookie cop would have recognized. The case was getting curiouser and curiouser all the time.

* * * *

Joe Costello had his client in my office at 9 a.m. sharp.

"Gat dag," Audie said, "Harvey-Dean had ta be shot four times. It was me, I'd 'o only needed one bullet ta kill him. I was in the Army…in Viet-Nam. I ain't no stranger ta guns."

I shook my head, immediately sick of his noise. "Let's quit bullshittin' each other, Audie. I didn't just fall off the turnip truck. I got your service records faxed here. You were what we in the regular Army called a *bo-lo*, a guy who couldn't qualify with his weapon. You were a lousy shot. In Vietnam, you were a supply clerk at 2nd Field Force headquarters in Long Binh. You spent your time in-country at the land of the big PX and a half dozen movie theatres. You never saw ten minutes of combat."

Joe Costello interrupted, "Sam, I've read the FBI report. Audie's fingerprints are all over the gun. So what? He owns it. But, there was one partial, unidentified print inside the trigger guard. Reasonable assumption someone else used the gun? Come on, Sam. The shooting was ten months ago."

Costello was certainly no legal slouch. His customers always got their money's worth.

"I take it your client has nothing more to say?" I asked. "He's not going to stand up like a man and tell the truth and take responsibility for his actions, for killing his son-in-law? Harvey-Dean was a guy who regularly beat your client's only daughter. Think about the possible defenses, Joe. He could plead guilty and still walk free."

Costello and his client mumbled a few words back and forth.

"Sorry, Sam, Audie says he had nothing to do with Harvey-Dean's death."

I shrugged. "Suit yourself. The next time we speak, there will be no deal in the wings for a cooperative defendant."

Costello turned both palms up. "Sam."

"Thanks for bringing him in, Joe."

As they left, Costello appeared a little embarrassed, and Audie, the miserable little runt, swaggered out, looking like he just defeated the entire legal system singlehanded.

I was about to express my frustrations to Bettye when I noticed an old woman sitting on one of the chairs in the reception area. Saying she was an old woman is an over-simplification. She could have been anywhere between fifty and a hundred-and-five. Her straight, gray hair extended down to her waist. She wore jeans, a pair of black Converse All-Star high-tops and a wool poncho—one just like the poncho my wife wore back in the 1960s. It was July, about 85 degrees outside, and not exactly weather for wool. I just couldn't wait to meet her.

"Chief," Bettye said, "this is Corsie Roberts. She'd like to see you."

Our visitor stood up. I gave her another once-over. She was very, very short.

"Hello, Ms. Roberts. Why don't you have a seat here at Sergeant Lambert's desk, and let's see how we can help you."

I glanced to the side at Bettye. Our eyes met. She rolled her eyes and made a face. I had no intention of doing that job alone.

Corsie Roberts sat in a side chair next to Bettye. I pulled up another chair and sat between them. She had a purse half the size of a GI duffle bag. She folded it on her lap and began to speak.

"Chief, this is so strange...I mean such a coincidence...my land. I came here to tell you about that man who just left."

"Which man was that?"

"Why, the evil one. That Audie Blevins, the one who runs the Arn Skellet."

"Runs the what?"

"The Arn Skellet—the place y'all raided over the weekend. They had pitchers on the TV."

"Oh, yes, the restaurant...sure."

Bettye rolled her eyes again.

"B'sides havin' those card games and sellin' that moonshine, that man's jest plain evil."

"Can you explain that to me, Ms. Roberts? Why do you call him evil?"

"Well, did I tell you I'm a'learnin' ta speak Cherokee?"

"No, ma'am, you sure didn't, but good for you."

"Well, I am. And...I live off Ellejoy Road, in that area that used ta be a Cherokee town long, long ago." She waited.

"Uh, huh. I know the area."

"Well, I believe I'm livin' rot over the ground where they buried their dead. And I've had some messages from the dead Cherokee folk." She narrowed her eyes and looked at me with an intensity I wouldn't have expected from her. "One man, a chief I'd say, told me the Blevins man was evil—him and his big white car."

An evil man with an evil Lincoln. "Yes, ma'am. Besides the gambling and the moonshine, have you seen any specific act of evil? Or have you been told about anything specific?"

She shook her head and looked pensive. "No, sir." More head shaking. "Not nothin' pacific I remember rot off. I thought I did, but...no, I jest know he is. Cain't remember why, but I jest know it."

"Wow, that's interesting, isn't it?" I said. "Deserves some lookin' into. I can't promise I'll do it myself, but I've got a few good men who will take care of this. If there's something to find, they'll find it."

She glanced at a wristwatch almost as large as an alarm clock. "Well, Lord have mercy," she said. "Look at what time it is. I don't want ta be late gettin' down ta Vonore for my Cherokee lessons." Then she lapsed into what might have been deep thought for a long moment. "Oh, for some reason I thought that evil man would be taller." She shrugged. "Oh, well."

"Yes, ma'am. We sure do appreciate your help identifying and locating the evil here in Prospect."

Corsie Roberts stood, looked at Bettye and then at me. She smiled and said, "Oh, she's so pretty, ain't she? I jest love her hair." Then she turned and left.

Bettye and I looked at each other. I shrugged.

"We appreciate your help locatin' the evil in Prospect? Are you ashamed of yourself, Sam Jenkins?"

"Jesus, Betts, what am I—a loon magnet? How do they all find me?" I genuinely needed to know.

"Before I go away and feel sorry for myself, be a good woman and rerun James 'Jammer' Begley through NCIC and anything else you can think of. His date of birth is on the statement from the other night. Junior came up with no hit on him for priors, but I noticed he had several tattoos that looked homemade—real jailhouse stuff. I'd be surprised if he's not in the system somewhere."

* * * *

I called Maryville PD and spoke with former county detective, now Assistant Chief Doyle Snoderly.

"All's I remember 'bout that case, shoot it was all the way back in Sep-tember last year, I think, was he's killed with four shots from a .45 automatic. Real professional-style. The shooter took the casins with him. I figured it was a contract hit."

His assessment went over with me like a lead balloon.

"The guy was a carpet installer—with no criminal affiliations. Who did you figure took out a contract on him?

"Cain't rightly say."

16

"I read the autopsy report. Only one of the four shots would have killed him. Not a very talented hit man. You think?"

Doyle invoked his right to remain silent.

"As a matter of fact, the gun was a revolver that used .45 automatic rounds in half-moon clips. There would have been no ejected casings. I found the gun. It's ninety-years-old…not exactly the weapon-of-choice for the serious assassin."

"Never seen a gun like that."

How in God's name did this moron get promoted to detective and then assistant chief of police?

"You know much about Audie Blevins, the guy I found in possession of the murder weapon? He's Harvey-Dean Mullins' father-in-law."

"Cain't say as I do."

"Harvey-Dean and his wife Dixie have a long history of domestic violence. You look at her as the killer?"

"Had an alibi."

"What was that?"

"Was with her momma."

"That sound believable to you? The story provided an alibi for Momma, too, didn't it?"

"Uh-huh. Didn't figger they'd lie. They's good Christian women."

"I'd better look for a lying atheist then. How about the old man? What did he have to say for himself?"

"Best I can remember, he could account fer his time, too."

Waste of valuable time. "Okay, Chief, thanks for your help."

The little voice inside me said, "Doyle Snoderly spoke with forked tongue."

* * * *

When Bettye returned from lunch, she handed me a short stack of paperwork on Jammer Begley and kept a single sheet for herself. We adjourned to my office and sat in the guest chairs in front of my desk. I slouched in one chair; Bettye sat with perfect posture and crossed her legs.

"James Lee Begley," she said, "twenty-seven years old, a number of arrests for drugs, a DUI, and he did three-hundred-and-sixty-four days for a house burglary. He's currently out on three years' supervised probation. He's got fourteen months to go."

I straightened up and tried to sound like Clark Gable when I said, "Frankly, my dear, I think you're a whiz with a computer."

She smiled. "Well, wasn't that a nice thing to say."

I waved the paperwork in the air as she stood to leave. "Thanks, kiddo. Let's see what ol' Jammer has to say for himself."

At 1:30, I called the home phone number Begley gave us the other night, thinking he might not yet be at work. I got lucky.

"Jammer, I understand you're a former guest of the Blount County correctional facility, and you're currently under the supervision of a probation officer."

"Yes, sir," he said, "and clean as a whistle since I's let go a year and a half ago."

"We need to talk, Jammer. What time do you start work today?"

"Four o'clock."

"Come on down to Prospect PD. I'll make this quick, and you'll be at the restaurant on time."

He agreed. Twenty minutes later, he sat in one of the saddle leather tan guest chairs in front of my desk. Jammer showed all the signs of a respectful ex-con: He sat at attention, hands resting on his thighs, looking me square in the eye.

"I'm not trying to screw you over, partner," I said, "but if I think you're giving me a run-around, I'll talk to your probation officer about you tending bar in an after-hours joint serving untaxed liquor and running an illegal card game. That's what we in the po-leece business call an unreputable establishment."

His deep frown told me I had hit a nerve. Jammer didn't look happy.

"Can I assume there's a stipulation to your parole about not associating with criminal elements?"

He nodded. "Yessir."

"What you tell me is confidential…for now. I won't intentionally cause you to lose your job, unless I lock up Audie Blevins, and they close the restaurant. I'll try my best to keep you out of this, but if it becomes necessary, I may need your testimony. Understand?"

He nodded again.

"Tell me about Audie, Dixie and Harvey-Dean."

Jammer didn't know much. He had seen Dixie showing signs of getting tuned up, he assumed, by her husband. He thought Harvey-Dean walked around with too much attitude for a skinny little guy and doubted he would have lasted thirty days in the county slammer. Jammer remembered that on several occasions Audie left the restaurant in a hurry after phone calls from Dixie. He never saw Audie leave with his handgun, but it was never locked up either. Dixie certainly had access to it. I believed what the kid told me.

So, I was ahead of the game, but not by much. I still wasn't sure I could lock down a good case against either Audie or Dixie.

* * * *

That night my wife and I were sitting at table 35 in the Villa Napoli. Kate was discussing a recipe for a pasta dish called Strozzapreti, which means priest stranglers in Italian, with Cervese sauce with Nick Cutrone, the restaurant owner. She spoke; he nodded. It all sounded good to me— shrimp, garlic, cubes of eggplant, cherry tomatoes, fresh basil, olive oil and oregano. Nick told her the closest he could get to Strozzapreti pasta was Casarecci. Kate understood and thought that would be satisfactory. I nodded, too. I was hungry.

Nick and I disagreed on the wine. I wanted a California Viognier. He suggested a Pinot Noir. He must have been hung up on the tomatoes. *Italians and their red wine.*

Nick disappeared and confirmed my suspicions that he had the hots for my wife when he changed the background music from Jerry Vale's portion of the album *Mob Hits* to Andrea Boccelli.

"Are you going to arrest that Blevins man for murder?" Kate asked.

"Soon maybe. His daughter could be good for it, too. I need to tie up a few lose ends first. He's got Joe Costello for his lawyer. No sense giving a sharp attorney an easy way to create reasonable doubt." I thought for a moment and shook my head. "I wish I could make this a slam-dunk. I've got the gun, but I can't put Audie at the scene as the shooter."

I finished speaking as Nick's grandson, Vinnie, the head bartender, brought our bottle of Viognier.

"No witnesses?" Kate asked when Vinnie left us.

"No one listed. I don't trust the detective who handled the case. I think some local politico got to him. I'll do another neighborhood canvas myself, but I don't have much hope. It happened last September. Most people can't remember what they ate for breakfast."

"Who was this woman you mentioned…the one who walked in claiming she had information?"

"No help. She was a space cadet." I shook my head in frustration. "All my life I've been like fly paper for crazies. Why me?"

"Even crazies can witness a crime, Sammy," she reminded me as she sipped her wine.

I nodded. "She did say two things that interested me. She knew Blevins owned a big white car. In fact, he owns a white Lincoln. And she said she thought the evil man—Blevins—was taller. I can't get that one out of my head. I wish I knew what that meant. Maybe I'll risk my sanity and go see her. She's nothing a couple of martinis wouldn't cure."

"You *should* see her again," Kate said.

"Wanna come along?"

"No!"

* * * *

First thing Monday morning, I hit the road and began knocking on doors along Ellejoy Road where Dixie Mullins lived and where Harvey-Dean had died. The area was rural with the homes spaced far apart. The air was warm, the sky a cloudless Caribbean blue.

A few neighbors told me that they had seen county sheriff's cars at the Mullins' home often enough, but no one remembered anything unusual or heard any shots that September day.

I took a deep breath and mustered up my intestinal fortitude for the drive toward Corsie Roberts' home. She lived on Country Lane, a narrow strip of blacktop lined by old deciduous trees off Ellejoy Road. Her place was a small, stick-framed house no bigger than a single-wide. An old brown Ford Maverick sat under a cluttered carport. A large plastic pot of marigolds stood next to her front door.

Corsie and her three cats answered the door and invited me in. I sat on the sofa. She wore an orange UT football jersey with big white double zeros on the back. The shirt was large enough to fit Stan Rose who's six-four and 235 pounds. Faded blue jeans and a pair of gold lame' flats showed below the jersey. Each of the marmalade-colored cats wore a different color, jewel-encrusted collar.

"Ms. Roberts, I spoke to several neighbors nearby and just couldn't find anyone who could add to what you told me about Mr. Blevins."

"Oh my, Chief, I am so surprised. Is there no one who can see through this evil man?"

"I've yet to find them."

"Will you keep tryin'?"

"I'd like to see if perhaps you could help me a little more."

"Why, yes, sir. I surely will try. I surely will. Before we speak more, would y'all like some herbal tea?"

I didn't want any, but thought it might put the old girl in a good mood. "Tea would be nice. Thanks."

She toddled off into the kitchen. The cats stayed behind to keep an eye on me. A big, burnt orange tom rubbed against my leg. I was glad I had worn khakis and not dark pants. I put my hand down to shoo him away. He rubbed his head against my hand. I picked him up and moved him two feet away. He turned and said, "Raaah!" and showed his fangs.

"Up yours," I said.

He sniffed, took a few steps away and stared at me.

Along one wall, three cat beds were lined up barracks fashion. Above them, perhaps twenty-four inches off the floor, three dream catchers were thumb tacked to the sheetrock. *Did Corsie buy her cats trinkets in the gift shop at the Cherokee Museum, or were they presents from the dead Indians who used to own the land?*

Corsie soon returned, and a few minutes later, we were sipping some horrid blend of chamomile and cat hair.

"You told me something about seeing Blevins' big car close by," I said. "He doesn't live in this neighborhood. Can you remember any more about that? Perhaps when or where you may have seen his car?"

That got a rise out of Corsie. She set her teacup down and bolted upright, slapping her right thigh. "Well, my land! I am so glad you asked. I have indeed been thinkin' 'bout that since I saw you last. My

21

land."

"Good. Was Mr. Blevins acting evil when you saw him and his car?"

She frowned at me, looking slightly disappointed. "Well, I should expect so. As I've said repeatedly, he is an evil man."

I gave a non-committal, "Uh-huh."

"What was it you asked just before?"

I refreshed her memory. "When did you see his car?"

"Oh, yes. It was Labor Day. Yes indeed…Labor Day last year."

"Where was the car and Mr. Blevins?"

She shook her head and made a face, as if she was attempting to explain something to a numbskull. "Why on Ellejoy Road, o' course. At the house jest before the Adams' Meadows subdivision."

That sounded like the Mullins' homestead to me.

"Why do you remember this happened on Labor Day?"

Her teacup clicked as she set it onto the saucer. "Well, sir, 'cause I was bound for the Sequoyah Birthplace Museum in Vonore. The very weekend after that they were havin' the annual powwow. I am on the volunteer committee, you know."

I gave her another encouraging smile. "I didn't know, but that's good. We narrowed down the date when you saw Blevins' car. Did you just see the car, or did you see Blevins himself?"

Corsie let out a huge volume of air—showing more frustration with the nitwit police chief. "Why, I saw both, o' course. That evil man come outta the house and walked towards his big white car parked in the driveway."

"You're sure it was Mr. Blevins?"

The fat cat had returned to rub his fur against my leg, and Corsie leapt into action. "Thaddeus, you bad boy. Don't be getting' fur on the Chief's pants leg. Shoo, now, shoo."

Thaddeus walked away, but not before giving me the evil eye. I wanted to stick out my tongue at him.

I repeated my question. "Were you certain it was Audie Blevins who walked to the car?"

She nodded thoughtfully. "Well, I believe so. Had that long, gray hair, tan pants and a brown sports coat. Looked taller though, taller than when I saw him at your po-leece station. I do expect evil people to be somewhat tall, don't you?" I guess she surprised herself with that remark. "Oh my, you're tall. But o' course I didn't mean to imply…"

"I understand. No offense taken." I smiled and took another sip of the cat urine she had served me. Why, I don't know. I wanted to spill it on Thaddeus's head. "Do you know about what time you may have seen this?"

She huffed again and let her shoulders rise and fall. "Well, o' course I do, Chief. I was due ta be at my committee meetin' at one o'clock. I always leave myse'f one hour ta drive ta Vonore. 'Course it only takes me forty-five or fifty minutes now that they've widened Route 411, but I leave one hour before. So, it would have been at jest about noon. Yes, sir, noon on Labor Day."

"Ms. Roberts, I surely do thank you. You're a sweetheart."

"Well, my land!"

* * * *

I checked my calendar. September 3rd had been Labor Day—the day Harvey-Dean Mullins was shot to death—with Audie Blevins' gun.

Back in the PD lobby, trying to sound as local as possible, I asked Bettye, "Whoaman, would ya far up yer com-puter an' run me a group search own Blevins? I'm a'needin' ta know how tawl Audie is."

"I shore will, Li'l Abner." She sounded a lot more country than usual.

"Li'l Abner? I can't believe you called me that." Then I did a better than average impersonation of Rodney Dangerfield. "No respect! I get no respect around here!"

"Sammy, that was really good. You sounded just like whatshisname."

"The late whatshisname. He was one of my favorite comedians. Anyway, while you're on the Blevins page at Motor Vehicles, see what you can find on a Mrs. Blevins."

A few moments later, she spun her chair around. "Here ya go, Sammy. Audie B. Blevins, DOB: 6-17-48 is five-foot six inches. Little feller, isn't he? He's got a Rockford address, and there's a LaRonda S. Blevins, 4-4-50, same address who's five-foot ten. That help you?"

I grinned. "Aha!"

"That good?"

"I think so. Let's hope they look alike."

"Do what?"

Next, I called Jackie Shuman.

"Your fingerprint technician find anything for me?"

"Shore did."

"Okay, you gonna tell me?"

"Shore will."

"Today?"

"I'm jest foolin' with ya, Sam. 'Course I'm gonna tell ya."

"Now?"

"Yer un-i-dentified fingerprint belongs to Dixie Mullins. Perty neat, huh?"

"Perty indeed. How'd you find her if the FBI couldn't?"

"Glad ya asked. She reported a house burglary back in 2004. The detective on the case had her come in fer a set of elimination prints. We kept 'em on file. Jest a six point match, but ol' Bert Lindsay, our fingerprint man, he says he'll swear there ain't no doubt."

"Didn't you tell me Bert Lindsay was a retired Chicago cop?"

"Yep, that's him. Been forty-eight years in law enforcement. Plans to retire with fifty."

"Lord have mercy. Thank him for me."

I love it when a plan comes together.

* * * *

I called Joe Costello.

"I believe we can wrap up this Harvey-Dean Mullins homicide quickly. Would you mind bringing your client into my office tomorrow at a reasonable hour?"

"'Course I will. Mind tellin' me what y'all have planned?"

"Well, I can't say you're going to like the outcome, but if Audie is willing to bring his wife and daughter with him, I believe we'll all see justice done. That work for you?"

"Do I still get paid?"

"Probably more than you think."

* * * *

On Tuesday at 10:30, Joe Costello led the procession of Blevinses into my office.

I had Officer Joey Gillespie come off the road to man the front desk so Bettye could join the festivities. What I had planned came straight out of a Nero Wolfe novel.

I brought in a pair of additional chairs from the lobby. Costello and Mrs. Blevins sat in my snazzy leather guest chairs while Audie and his daughter planted themselves in the lobby seats. Bettye sat to the right of my desk on an armless side chair.

"Okay, Mr. Blevins," I said, "I think this whole affair has dragged on long enough. Before I arrest you for the murder of Harvey-Dean Mullins, I'll make my offer of a deal for leniency once more. You confess and sign a statement your attorney approves, and I'll see that the district attorney works with you. What do you say?"

He and Costello put their heads together and mumbled between themselves. Audie was doing a lot of head shaking. When they broke the huddle, Audie spoke.

"I done tole ya," he said, raking a hand through his thick, long, gray hair. "I ain't kilt Harvey-Dean. How many times I got ta say it?"

"You sure about this? Last chance."

He shook his head and was about to speak when I interrupted, "Joe, is your client giving his final word?"

Joe shrugged. He didn't look as if he agreed with Audie's decision. "I guess he is."

"So, he claims to be innocent?"

Costello frowned, looking unsure what I'd do next. "He does."

I stood abruptly. "Okay, Sergeant Lambert, put your cuffs on Dixie Mullins, and arrest her for the murder of her husband, Harvey-Dean."

"What?" Dixie spoke with genuine shock in her voice.

She looked like a younger version of her mother, tall, but thinner with platinum blonde hair.

"The previously unidentified fingerprint on the murder weapon has been identified as yours. You're under arrest."

"Dixie, I advise you to say nothin'." Costello said.

"Joe, I see a possible conflict of interest here. Do you represent Audie or Dixie? I still think Audie's lying. You can't represent both people. If Dixie didn't kill her husband and flips on her father, you can't play both roles."

"Flip on my father? What's that mean?" Dixie looked confused...and frightened.

"Dixie," I explained, "it means if you know your daddy killed Harvey-Dean and you didn't, you can save yourself at least twenty-five years in jail by telling me how your daddy did it."

"I don't know what you're talkin' about," she squawked.

Bettye had walked around my desk and now stood behind Dixie with a set of handcuffs in her right hand.

"Okay, works for me. Sergeant, read Dixie her rights, and take her to the squad room for processing."

"Wait! Jest wait!" LaRonda Blevins sprang to her feet. "You can't prove either Audie or Dixie killed that man."

LaRonda stood next to Audie, four inches taller than him. She had dressed in a masculine outfit, a pair of khaki Dockers, New Balance cross trainers and a light blue, man-tailored, button-down shirt. Her hair was gray like her husband's, longer than his by a little, but short for a woman.

"We'll see what a jury says, Mrs. Blevins. I have a better than fair circumstantial case against Dixie. Your husband denies any involvement, and I can't with certainty place him at the scene. I have a gun that Dixie had access to, but had no reason to be in possession of. Her fingerprint is on that gun. It undoubtedly killed her husband—the guy who beat her on a regular basis. Ask Mr. Costello. Have people been convicted with less?"

Joe nodded.

"Remember what you hear on TV cop shows: motive, means and opportunity? She had all three. I've got the murder weapon. End of story."

"You'd put my daughter in jail after that...man beat her and degraded her day in and day out?"

"Yes ma'am. All part of the job." I cracked a slight smile.

She looked from Audie to Dixie to Costello. Thankfully, Joe

remained silent.

"Wait…jest wait," she said again.

She stared at me. I waited.

"All right. All right," she said. "Leave her alone. I know what you're after. All right. I shot him. You damn well know I shot him, don't ya?"

It was my turn to remain silent. I stared into her eyes, hoping the silence would annoy her. In a moment, she blinked first and spoke again.

"I killed Harvey-Dean to keep him from harmin' my daughter any more. Can you blame me?"

"Do you want to have an attorney present before you say any more?" I asked.

"I want you to please leave my daughter alone."

"Joe," I said, "Mr. Blevins may wish to dismiss you from his employ. Would you care to represent Mrs. Blevins?"

Costello nodded.

"Do you think she'd accept the same magnanimous deal I offered her husband? A confession for my assurance you and she can negotiate a reasonable plea bargain with Moira Menzies?"

They spoke in hushed tones for a few seconds.

"That works for us," he said. "You won't oppose any deal Moira offers?"

"It's hard to believe that the other two didn't know all the details and aren't complicit in this whole business, but I have a heart. Make your deal. I'll work with Detective Stallins and help him close out the case. Moira has her own investigators if she wants to pursue Audie and Dixie for accessorial conduct. I'm happy with what I've gotten."

Costello nodded his agreement. LaRonda was ready to start writing her confession.

* * * *

Kate, Bettye and I were sitting at one of the dozen tables in Wah Lum, the Chinese restaurant on the town square in Prospect. The owner, Mr. Lum, was taking our orders while we all sipped hot jasmine tea. Kate ordered Dragon & Phoenix. I chose noodles with spicy peanut sauce and shrimp. Bettye said she wanted sweet and sour pork.

"No!" Mr. Lum said. "Miss Bettye, you order sweet and sour pork, sweet and sour pork, all the time sweet and sour pork. Today you order something else."

Bettye looked at me.

"Sounds reasonable to me," I said with a smile. "Don't be a creature of habit."

She looked at Kate for an ally. Kate shrugged.

Mr. Lum waited, pad in hand.

"You like nuts?" I asked.

"Nuts?"

"Yeah. Nuts. Cashews?"

"Sure, I guess," Bettye said.

"Chicken with cashews, Mr. Lum," I said. "Miss Bettye would like chicken with cashews."

"Oh, good choice, Mr. Sam. Very good choice. I make extra good for Miss Bettye."

He scurried away and we were back to sipping our tea.

"Can you believe that?" Bettye said.

"The old guy thinks of himself as a culinary artist. He wants you to try new things."

Bettye shrugged and asked, "How did you sort this one out, Sam?"

"A couple of old cats told me."

THE END

A Murder in Knoxville

Wayne Zurl

A Murder in Knoxville
Wayne Zurl

If I knew how to deal with women, I wouldn't get involved with some of the things that cause me trouble. I was minding my own business, trying to be just another small-town cop when the phone rang. Caller ID showed the number of my favorite TV reporter.

"Well, hello there." She sounded very sexy.

"Hi, how're you today?"

"I'm doing just fine, and I'm glad you're in the office."

"You sound like you're in a good mood this morning," I said.

"I am. I'm in the mood for love. Want to have phone-sex?"

I think I'm a pretty worldly guy, but that one threw me for a loop.

"Rachel, sweetheart, you're my best friend, but the last time I looked we were married—and not to each other. You know I try to be good where you're concerned. So, how can you ask me that? You have no mercy."

"You are so cute when you get flustered."

"I am not flustered."

"Are, too."

"Jeez," I said, "did you hear yourself? That was so jejune."

"Jejune?"

"Yeah, it means…"

"I know what it means," she interrupted. "No one on earth says *jejune* except you."

"That's not true. If I didn't want to behave myself, I'd rent a movie, and we could watch an old Woody Allen film where they use the word more than once."

"If you take me to that drive-in near Prospect, I'll make out with you."

"Will you cut that out?"

"Well, if you won't take advantage of my invitations, I'd better get down to business."

"You just want to stop this R-rated dialogue and talk business without skipping a beat? Is that any way to treat your buddy?"

"Oh, I love this. Little Rachel can turn her big tough-guy into an old softie."

"Lady, you won't get me to comment on that one. No ma'am, not me."

"I think you just did, Sammy. Were you getting hot and bothered?"

"You're a shameless hussy."

"Oh, you're so sweet. You're the only man I'd ever leave home for."

"Where have I heard that line before?"

"Well, it's true. Now, if you won't make love to me over the phone, we have to talk seriously. Will you do me a favor?"

"Of course I'll do you a favor. Silly woman. You could have just asked instead of making me need a cold shower."

"Do I have that effect on you?"

"Stop fishing. What do you want?"

"It's really not for me. One of the assistant producers, Angie Valle—I think you've met her—is having a problem."

"What's wrong?"

"I need to ask something first. How do you feel about arresting another police officer?"

That's the kind of thing a cop never likes to hear, but occasionally you do.

"I've had to do that before when I worked in New York. Look, cops generally don't like to lock up other cops, but if it's necessary, I can deal with that."

"Okay, good. Angie's separated from her husband, a Knoxville policeman. He's threatened her."

"He's a Knoxville city cop?

"Yes."

"Where does Angie live?"

"In Fountain City."

"That's Knox County's area. I can't do something that far away. Police work is like the garbage collection business. The local wise guys dictate who picks up trash in designated areas. Cops have their own turf. We don't go into other districts unless we connect it to a crime where we work."

"I know all that, Sammy. I just thought since he lives in Prospect now, you could have a talk with him."

"Aha!" I said.

"Aha?"

"Yes, aha. The plot thickens."

"Don't be melodramatic."

"You want me to act as Angie's hired muscle."

"No, I don't. Well, maybe, sort of. She doesn't really want to have him arrested. I only thought that you could have a talk with him. You know, as one policeman to another."

"Are you going to tell me the story, or is Angie?"

"She's right here. I'll put her on."

"Wait a minute, woman. Has she been there all the time we've been talking?"

"Uh-huh."

"She heard what you said to me?"

"Yes, she did."

"Jeez. It's like being filmed having sex."

"Oh, don't be such a prude."

"My life was not this complicated until I met you."

"I know, Lover. You're so sweet. Here talk to Angie."

* * * *

Rachel Williamson is the evening newscaster on a Knoxville TV station. I'm the police chief in a small town just south of Tennessee's third largest city. Angie Valle worked at Rachel's station.

I've never been able to figure out the difference between a producer and an executive producer or an associate producer and a supervising producer or any of that technical television business. With all the other complications Rachel creates in my life, I've never had the courage to ask.

Angela Valle explained that she and her estranged husband, Howie Wetzel, had separated nine months earlier. Because of irreconcilable differences, she had no intention of reuniting. Howie, on the other hand, wanted her back—badly.

In the last six months, Angie had gone out with several other men— each of them visited by Howie and warned to stay away from his wife, two of them at gunpoint. Some cops believe they can stretch the rules of good behavior to solve a personal problem.

Wetzel currently remained on disability leave after an on-duty traffic accident, claiming he suffered incurable whiplash. He'd hired an attorney to get him classified as officially disabled and entitled to a line-of-duty disability pension.

I learned that Howie was originally from Cincinnati. He had taken the job with Knoxville PD seven years earlier when he left the Army after serving three years in the Military Police Corps.

Howie lived in the Foot O' the Mountains Mobile Home Park on the outskirts of my city, beautiful downtown Prospect. Fool that I am, I agreed to talk some sense into the man.

After taking care of a few of the necessities needed to run a small police department, I had lunch and then drove to the trailer park, hoping to speak rationally with Officer Wetzel.

A late model Nissan Z-370 was parked at the foot of a relatively new single-wide on Song Bird Lane. I knocked at the door and met a man in his early thirties. If Howie hadn't been a cop, he could have gotten a job modeling in a police supply catalog. He looked to be about five-foot-ten and could have worn a perfect size forty-regular. His short dark hair and startling blue eyes would no doubt attract the ladies—until they got to know him.

After a few minutes of chatting with Howie, I started to have serious doubts about Knoxville's psychological screening process. Howie struck me as an unleashed shit-house rat.

"Are you here to charge me with a crime?" he asked, bristling with attitude.

"I'm here as a favor to your ex-wife and as a courtesy to you—as one cop to another. I'm an impartial observer. But from experience, I can tell you that putting the arm on Angela's new friends will get you jammed up with your job and possibly tossed into the Knox County court system. If you think about it for a while, you'd see that."

"Oh, you're saying I don't see things clearly? You saying I'm a psycho or something?" His attitude went from bad to worse.

"I'm telling you nothing more than what you heard. I have no vested interest here. My friend works with your ex-wife. And your ex is on the verge of taking legal action against you." I paused to let the idea sink in. "Hey, you're looking for a disability pension worth big bucks to you. I'm only suggesting you put your efforts into getting that tax-free pension rather than into tracking down her boyfriends and breaking their balls. However, you can still collect a pension while you're doing hard time. Your choice."

No one will ever accuse Howie of having the ability to hide his unspoken thoughts. He used more body language in those few moments than a mime.

"Look," I said, losing patience myself, "do whatever you want. If you break the law in Prospect, I'll lock up your ass—cop or not. Other than that, fend for yourself. Thanks for your time." I turned and left.

Before I got into my car, I looked at Howie standing in his doorway and heard him saying, "Yeah, thanks for stopping by. Tell my ex thanks a bunch for sending one of the farm-cops to see me. Have a nice day, asshole."

* * * *

That was Wednesday. The next Monday morning, I received a call from a Knoxville PD lieutenant named Claude Sturgill. He told me he worked in their Internal Affairs section.

Sturgill explained that late Saturday night, Howie kicked in the door to Angie's apartment and found her with a new boyfriend. When the friend didn't respond to Howie's demand to leave, Howie took out his department issue Glock and hit the man on the side of his head.

Quick to learn that he was out-gunned, the boyfriend retreated to his car, but didn't leave without calling the county deputies. Prior to the arrival of the sheriff's men, Howie smacked Angie a few times to show his affection and then left.

Angie may have been reluctant to sign a complaint against her ex, but the new boyfriend wanted his pound of flesh. Lieutenant Sturgill had a warrant charging Officer Wetzel with aggravated assault and a personnel order, signed by his chief, to confiscate Wetzel's guns.

Sturgill showed courtesy by telling me he wanted to execute a warrant in my jurisdiction. He went a little further by asking me to assist.

"None of the squad detectives want ta lock up a brother officer," he said. "I've got no help with me today. I hope ya don't mind lendin' a hand here."

"I have no problem with that. I've met Wetzel. He has the personality of a moray eel. Getting collared might give him a little humility and may do the prick some good."

The arrest went off without incident, unless you count Wetzel telling Lieutenant Sturgill not to smoke in his trailer. Reluctantly, Wetzel surrendered four handguns, three of which were listed on departmental records and one that was owned 'under the table', so to speak.

Sturgill declined my offer to drive to Knoxville with him. He cuffed Wetzel like any other defendant and belted him into the back seat behind the cage that divided his unmarked police car.

After Sturgill left Prospect, I called Rachel Williamson.

"Do Angie a favor, and convince her to lock her doors and put 9-1-1 on speed-dial," I said. "Stress the idea that she should not deal with this guy personally, and don't, for God's sake, let him into her apartment."

"Okay, Sammy."

"I'm just guessing here, Rachel, but he probably holds her responsible for him being jammed up at work. These guys never think any of this is their fault. If Howie finds out he's getting the sack over this incident, who knows what he'll do."

"Do you think Angie is in serious danger?" Rachel asked.

"She could be. Wetzel is neither a nice guy nor a happy camper."

"What should she do? I mean in the long run."

"My suggestion is to start with a long vacation. That would allow time for Knoxville PD and the court to settle up with Howie. If that's not possible, keep the phone handy and call 9-1-1 if he shows up anywhere near her. An order of protection from the court would be nice, but who knows if he'd respect it? I doubt he would."

"Sam, I really appreciate your help with this. I don't know how I can thank you."

"How about unlimited phone-sex for a year?" I suggested.

"Oh, oink."

Did I say something distasteful?

"Hey," I said, "that was your idea, not mine."

* * * *

After being released on minimum bail, Wetzel paid Angie a visit Wednesday night. Not being one to take my good advice, Angie allowed Howie into her apartment. Among the other meaningful things he told her, he stressed that if she decided on having future relationships with members of the opposite sex, he would terminate her existence. After Howie stormed out into the night, Angie again called the sheriff's department to make a report. Then she called Rachel, and Rachel called me at home with this information. I suggested that Angie telephone the Knoxville PD duty officer and have him interrupt Lieutenant Sturgill's evening.

The next day Sturgill called me.

"Our boy Wetzel was out on the town again last night," he said. "Paid his ex a visit and made some more threats. I'd like ta go see the judge and git his bail revoked."

"You think your chief is going to fire him?"

"I suspect so, but I gotta see what he says. Anyways, I gotta ask him if I can get Howie put inta jail."

"Locking Wetzel up is easier than a twenty-four hour security detail watching his ex-wife. I don't know where Wetzel's head is, except up his ass, but it seems like he just can't help himself."

He chuckled. "I hear that."

"If you need me to help with another arrest, just whistle."

"Okay, I'll call ya."

Just to update me, Sturgill did call back. His chief thought with the pending court case, it was improbable that Wetzel would either contact or do any further harm to Angie. He told Sturgill to leave Wetzel alone.

In all the years I've spent in law enforcement, one of my greatest failings has been a jealousy toward high-ranking police officers who were given access to those magical crystal balls allowing them to see the future. I never could find one.

* * * *

At 1:30 Thursday morning, my home phone rang. Katherine, my wife, awoke first and shook me.

"Sam, the phone's ringing. It's probably for you."

"Okay," I said, my mouth thick and bad-tasting.

I walked into the adjoining room where we kept the upstairs phone.

On the line I heard, "This Chief Sam Jenkins from Prospect PD?"

"Yeah, who's this?"

"Name's Wendell Hatmaker, detective with Knox County." He pronounced his name as if he spelled it Windell.

"Uh-huh, what's up?"

Had I been more awake, I would have guessed.

"Sorry ta be wakin' ya, but I'm investigatin' a homicide up in Fountain City. Woman named Angela Valle was beat ta death. I found yer business card in her pockabook. You got some connection with my victim?"

I took a deep breath. "Yeah, she works with a friend. She's been having lots of trouble with her ex-husband, a Knoxville city cop. He lives in Prospect."

"Your friend named Rachel?"

"Yeah, how'd you know that?"

"Her name and number's on the back o' yer card."

"You like her ex for this?" I asked, not at all surprised.

"Don't rightly know yet. Ain't nobody callin' in ta confess."

"What can I do for you?"

"How 'bout he'pin' me find this ex-husband?"

"Sure, I'll send a couple guys to his place and wake him up. If he's home, we'll have him available for you. If he's not, send a couple of men to watch his trailer until he gets there. Your guys can call the Blount County dispatcher when they get to Prospect, and a car will meet them. Let me have your number so my cops can call you one way or the other."

I wrote down the two numbers he gave me.

"Mind if I take a drive down ta yer neck o' the woods tomorra anyways? Jest so we can compare notes, so ta speak?"

"Sure, I'm in at nine o'clock. How early do you want to get there?"

"How 'bout 10:30 or 11:00? I'll need me some beauty sleep afta workin' this all night."

"Okay, I'll be there."

"Night now," he said.

When Hatmaker hung up, I called one of the on-duty Prospect cops and told him what to do and how to touch base with the Knox County deputies. I later learned that Howie Wetzel was MIA.

I went back to bed and hit the mattress like a cargo bundle kicked out of the tailgate of a C-130.

"Easy, big feller," Kate said. "That's a hundred-and-eighty pounds hitting the springs."

I grunted to show my displeasure. "I hate getting up like this. I'll never get back to sleep."

"Sure you will, Sammy. Just relax, and don't be mad."

"Not that easy."

Kate turned to face me.

"I know what will put you to sleep."

I felt her hand on my thigh.

"Oh yeah? How can you be so sure?"

"After all the years we've been married, I'd bet one of your pension checks that right after we make love I'll put my head on your shoulder, and we'll both be asleep in no time."

"Even if it didn't work we'd be fools not to try."

"That's right, sweetie. Now why don't you lose those PJs?"

* * * *

I parked my car in the lot of the municipal building at ten-to-nine the next morning. Before I could walk into the PD, Rachel called my cell phone. I spent almost thirty minutes on the phone with her talking about Angie's murder. Hatmaker woke her up a few minutes after he finished with me.

At 11:00, Detective Wendell Hatmaker walked into my office. He extended his hand and re-introduced himself.

"Howdy. Windell Hatmaker at yer service. Most folks jest call me

Windy, like the hamburger place," he said.

He looked around fifty-years-old, about five-foot-ten and fifteen to twenty pounds overweight. He had wavy red hair, streaked with gray and combed straight back. His clothes looked like he found them in the Good Will store on half-price day. But Windy Hatmaker was one of the happiest-looking guys I can remember meeting.

Windy and I used my car to visit Howie Wetzel, only Howie still hadn't come home. The two Knox County deputies were still there; one asleep and the other barely alive, but with his eyes open. It had been a long night for them.

We began a neighborhood canvas and interviewed a woman who had seen Wetzel drive away in his black Z-370 at approximately 10 a.m. the day before. Things were not looking any better for old Howie.

Before returning to Knoxville, Windy and I stopped at Howell's Pub for lunch. He enjoyed an award-winning barbeque pork sandwich, and I had the opportunity to ask questions.

"You mind if I take a look at your crime scene?" I said.

"Ain't mine no more," he said. "We're finished. He'p ya se'f. Don't know whatcha gonna find. We had the crime scene guys work it over real good."

"I don't know that I'd find anything. I just like to re-visit crime scenes. I met Wetzel—not for long, but I think I've got a handle on him. I don't know…sometimes when I look at a scene I get sort of a…feeling for what happened. It's hard to explain."

Windy licked the barbeque sauce off his fingers and put down the sandwich.

"Well, I'll be." He rubbed a napkin over his hands. "Shore, give it a go. Ya know, I'll be honest with ya. I called a friend at Blount County an' asked about ya. They think yer a good man. Told me ya came from one o' them big departments on Long Island. Now jest where is Long Island?"

"Look at it as the appendix of New York City. It sticks out into the Atlantic to the east. It used to be nice, before all the city people moved there to live near the beaches. Now if you don't count the boroughs of Brooklyn and Queens, there are more than three million people on a strip of land at most fourteen miles wide. A real crowded place. Makes a cop's life pretty busy."

"Ain't that somethin'? Three million people. Almost as many as in all o' Tennessee." He shook his head and looked amazed. "Them Blount County boys think ya like ta work things alone, but ya git results. So, shore, go an' look all ya want. I'll take all the he'p I kin git."

"Another favor?" I asked. "I'd like the name of Ms. Valle's boyfriend, the one Howie tuned up and the names of the cops who answered the calls at her place."

"Okey dokey, I'll git 'em fer ya'." Windy smiled and took a long drink of his sweet tea.

* * * *

Later that afternoon, I followed Detective Hatmaker back to the Knox County Sheriff's Department, picked up the keys to Angie Valle's apartment and drove north alone on Broadway into the middle-class community of Fountain City. The apartment made up one-sixth of a two-story brick building, each unit having its own door facing the tree-lined street. Older brick homes, private single-family residences, surrounded the small apartment house. I unlocked the door to Angie's place.

Traces of fingerprint powder remained on many surfaces within the apartment. Any fool could see this had been a major crime scene. As I looked over the living room, I began reconstructing the incident. From the photos I had seen, I knew that the assailant struck Angie on the front right side of her head. To me that said a left-handed attacker. I had noticed Howie Wetzel was right handed. She fell to her left and struck her temple on the corner of a glass-topped coffee table. That undoubtedly killed her.

I envisioned an accidental murder—perhaps manslaughter—because of the reckless act of hitting a one-hundred-and-twenty-pound woman with brute force. Establishing a killer's intent can be difficult unless they run down the street screaming, "I'm gonna kill ya!" In attempting to obtain a confession, having the lesser charge of manslaughter available to fall back on might convince a suspect to cut his losses and cop a plea while the offer sat on the table. Anyway, it's a good theory.

Everything indicated that the crime scene technicians had done a thorough job. In the once nearly spotless apartment, I found nothing of interest. I moved to the kitchen—still nothing but the usual toaster, blender, microwave and other assorted gadgets.

Then on a whim, I opened the sliding glass door that led out to a small deck off the breakfast nook. I saw two plastic chairs and a short round table. Conspicuously absent was the barbeque grill almost every other resident of East Tennessee owns. I continued to look around and noticed something under the lower 2 x 4 rail wedged against the upright post—a matchbook. I thought that odd. I saw no ashtrays either inside or on the deck. A few candles were scattered throughout the rooms, but a Scripto propane candlelighter sat on a kitchen counter to take care of those.

I picked up the matchbook and saw it came from a restaurant and bar on Kingston Pike in Knoxville, a popular watering hole with the after work crowd. When I opened the cover, I noticed that most of the matches had been used, but had not been torn from the book. Instead, they were bent. It took an acquired talent to strike a bent match with one hand and not set the rest of the book afire.

I remembered my stepfather could do it. He told me he learned how in the Navy during World War II. A sailor didn't want to get caught throwing spent matches on the deck. As a kid, I tried to master the skill, but only ended up with a fist full of fire.

I wondered who left the matchbook. Howie Wetzel didn't smoke. He made an issue about cigarettes when Sturgill wanted to light up.

I dropped the matchbook into a little Zip-Loc bag and put it in my jacket pocket. I walked from the deck back into the apartment and then upstairs to Angie's bedroom.

My cell phone rang.

"This is Officer Curtis Fouts, Knox County," the caller said. "Windy Hatmaker said y'all wanna talk ta me."

"Yeah, thanks for calling. Windy probably told you I'm helping out in Angela Valle's murder investigation. We're looking at her ex-husband for that. He lives in my jurisdiction. I wonder if I could speak with you in person about what you saw when you answered those calls at her place."

"I done tol' ever'thin' that happened ta Windy already."

"I know you did, and I'm sorry to bother you, but I know the suspect, and Windy doesn't. If it's not too much trouble, could you meet me at the victim's apartment?"

"I ain't got a call rot now. I kin be there in ten minutes. That work?"

"Sure it does, and I appreciate it. The other man, Vance Lonis, who came here with you when Howie Wetzel assaulted Angie's boyfriend…is he working now?"

"Vance is off t'day. Somebody else is workin' his area. You'll have ta catch him another time."

"Okay, I'll see you in ten minutes."

When Curtis Fouts arrived, he entered the apartment without knocking. Immediately, I felt pleased to have tied up with him. I never needed to ask a question. I looked at him, sized him up and watched his actions. I knew I had found Angie Valle's killer.

The first thing I noticed was the service pistol on his left side. When he got close to me, I smelled nicotine on his uniform.

Fouts looked like a real lounge lizard—what cops call a swordsman. I had known dozens of his type back in New York; cops who loved to work the swing shift. After they finished work late at night, they went directly to some gin mill or cheater's lounge trolling for chicks.

A tattoo of a fouled anchor on his right forearm showed below the short sleeve of his uniform shirt; USN written above the anchor's eyelet and USSJFK below the flukes. Fouts had been a sailor on an aircraft carrier.

After we spoke for several minutes, he sealed his fate. His account of the domestic problems that took place in the apartment sounded concise and professional, but while he told me the story, he took out a soft-pack of Marlboros and a book of safety matches. With one hand, he bent a match and rubbed the head over the abrasive striker. Voila, the match burned. He lit the cigarette and blew out the flame

Guys like Fouts were predators in their own right. I knew their kind. Other cops knew them, too. They'd answer a call where a female had been assaulted or otherwise victimized by a husband or boyfriend. The women were upset; they were vulnerable. Then shortly after he finished work, the chivalrous 'blue knight' who answered the woman's earlier summons would return.

"Are you all right?" he might ask.

"Yes, thanks for asking," she would reply.

"I was concerned for your safety," he'd say with a caring smile.

"Were you? That's very sweet," she would respond.

The pair exchanged more words.

Depending on the woman's susceptibility and the amount of silver coating on the cop's tongue, he may get beyond first base.

Often they did. I know this because the day after, they'd brag about it. Some cops rarely respect the don't kiss and tell rule.

Confronting Fouts with my suspicions would have been foolish. Anyone with his experience would only deny my allegation. I needed more evidence before I could nail him. It would take time, and I'd want to use another favorite investigative technique of mine—be at the crime scene at the precise time the incident occurred. In this case, that meant sometime around midnight.

But who wants to work those hours alone? I needed a partner. I couldn't ask one of my cops to work in Knoxville without compensation, and I couldn't put someone on overtime while in another jurisdiction. I didn't want to ask Windy Hatmaker. After all, this was his case, and he might want to call the shots. I needed an amateur sleuth who enjoyed my company. I used my cell phone.

"How'd you like your favorite gumshoe to buy you dinner tonight?"

"I'd love it. What's the occasion?"

"I need a partner. I'm on that case in Knoxville, and I want a good pair of eyes to watch my back. And it's going to be late when we finish this, so I need someone to keep me awake."

"Lucky me," she said.

"Why complain? Did I call someone else? Don't I trust you most? You get dinner and the opportunity to work with one of the world's greatest detectives."

"Yeah, yeah, yeah."

Women seem to love my modesty.

Then I allowed Peter Sellers to pitch my idea.

"Listen to me, Cato. The case I have been working, it is now solved. I have only to amass more evi-donce and then use my old interrogation ploy, and the villain, he will crumble before me."

"Oh, Inspector Clouseau, you are brilliant." She tried to sound

Oriental.

"*Chief Inspector*, my little, yellow friend. I will pick you up at eight o'clock. We shall drive north of the city, eat a scrumptious re-past and then begin our sur-val-lonce. Be ready, Cato. Crime waits for no one."

"You know, you're nuts," she said, again using her own voice. "And what am I for staying married to you all these years?"

"Hey, plenty of women would kill to have dinner with me."

"Who?"

* * * *

After a leisurely and expensive meal at Chesapeake's and then a quick drive up Broadway, at 10 p.m. we sat in my Crown Victoria in front of Angie's apartment.

We waited and waited, for what I wasn't sure. A jogger, a walker, lovers who stroll in the moonlight—someone who may have passed that way the night Angie was killed. I hoped for a creature of habit to get caught in my web.

At 11:45, I looked in the side mirror and saw a woman walking our way with a dog on a leash.

"Bingo," I said to Kate. "Here's a good possibility coming at us. Get out of the car when I do. Let her see a woman's with me when I speak to her. You may keep her from getting spooked."

"You've got it, boss. I'm right behind you."

The dog-walker stood twenty yards behind our car when we got out. A brindle and white greyhound sniffed the base of a tree. I crossed the road with my badge in hand.

"Excuse me, ma'am," I said. "I'm a police officer. May I speak to you?"

She stopped short. I noticed she wore one of those 'nouveau nurse' outfits consisting of shocking-pink baggy pants, a wildly printed, shapeless top and a pair of puce-colored Crocs. At the end of her leash, the jittery greyhound, looking for a place to lift his leg, fidgeted.

"Don't come any closer!" she said. "Stay where you are. I've got pepper spray!" She spoke louder than necessary.

"Take it easy. I don't mean you any harm. I'm a cop."

Kate came to stand next to me.

"I just want to ask you a question about a crime that took place here the other night."

"Okay, but no fast moves. Walk under the street light where I can see you."

Kate and I moved twenty feet to our left and stood under the mercury bulb, just as the woman requested. I showed her my badge again.

"Anybody can get a piece of tin like that. Let's see some photo ID."

Careful is good, but I do not look like a criminal.

"It's in my wallet. Back, left pocket. I'm getting it now."

I really didn't want a face full of Mace.

"Right, let's see it. Slow and careful."

She sounded more like a cop than me. I showed her my ID card.

"Thanks. Can't be too careful, you know."

I nodded, but wanted to give her the raspberries. "Sure. Good idea."

"I just finished a three-to-eleven in the ER at St. Mary's. I walk Fortunato every night when I get home," she said.

I returned the wallet to my pocket.

"Fortunato?"

"Yeah, I got him from Greyhound Rescue. I figure he was lucky. Me too…he's a good dog."

"You don't sound like a local, Ms…?"

"Ensslin, Suzanne Ensslin. No, I'm from Morristown, New Jersey. How about you? You sound like Nu Yawk."

"You've got a good ear. Yeah, I'm originally from Long Island."

"I thought so. So, whaddaya need to know?"

Nurse Ensslin sounded like a real piece of work.

"Around this time Wednesday night or early Thursday morning, the woman who lived across the street was murdered. 9-1-1 got a call from a neighbor at 12:10, saying they heard a fight. The neighbor phoned the girl and got no answer. Did you and Fortunato walk around here that night?"

"Yeah, like I said, every night—same time."

"Did you see anything or anybody on the street? A vehicle perhaps?"

"You said 9-1-1 got a call *after* midnight?"

"Correct. 12:10."

"That's weird. Unless I work overtime, I get here before midnight. I did that night, and I saw a cop-car parked over there."

"What kind of police car?"

"A marked county sheriff's car."

"Anyone in the car?"

"No."

"You're sure it was before midnight?"

"Positive. I got home, heard my clock chime twelve times, and then I watched the rest of Jay Leno. No doubt about it."

"You didn't happen to see a number on the car, did you?"

"Sure I did. I notice stuff like that. It had 721 on the rear plate. I could see it from the street light."

"Thanks, Ms. Ensslin. That was very helpful. One more question—do you really have pepper spray?"

"You bet—cocked and locked—whole can full."

"Good for you. Thanks for your help."

* * * *

The next morning, I made it a priority to find the elusive Howie Wetzel. I started with a call to Claude Sturgill.

"You've probably heard Wetzel's ex-wife was killed late Wednesday," I said.

He told me he had.

"Knox County is still looking at him as their first choice," I said, "but I did some work on my own, and I think someone else looks better. I want to find Howie and see if he's got a credible alibi."

"Uh-huh," Sturgill said. "Whatcha need me ta do"

"Neither he nor his car has been seen since before the murder. Can you give me any names up in Ohio where he still has ties?"

"You're a real one-man band, ain't ya?"

"Just a motivated soloist. While you're looking for Cincinnati phone numbers, can you check if he's listed any new paramour as an alternate place of contact?"

"Para who?"

"Goomah, squeeze, girlfriend." I clarified *paramour*.

"Oh, sure. You folks from New York do talk a funny language."

"You should hear it when a couple of us get together."

"No thanks. Hang on now. I'll be rot back."

I waited ten minutes without the benefit of Musak. Then Lieutenant Sturgill came back with a little information. Wetzel's mother's address and phone number were available. He listed a sister from Florence, Kentucky as the person to contact in case of an emergency. Florence is just south of the Ohio River, but still part of metro-Cincinnati. I called Mommy first.

"Mrs. Wetzel, my name is Jenkins. I'm with the police department in Prospect, Tennessee…the city where your son lives."

"Yes."

She spoke without emotion and never asked if her son was all right. A cop's mother, or any family member, who gets a phone call from a PD, usually expects bad news and questions it.

"Mrs. Wetzel, believe it or not, I'm calling to keep your son out of more trouble than he's already gotten himself into. I know he's there with you. Put him on the phone, please."

I heard nothing but silence.

"Mrs. Wetzel, please, if you lie to me I'll just send the Cincinnati Police there and someone to your daughter's house in Florence. They won't leave any of you alone until I find Howie."

More silence, then after a long moment, a new party entered the conversation. "What are you callin' me here for?"

I recognized the voice.

"Lose the attitude, Howie." I let my annoyance show, too. "I can always have the local cops pick you up for violating your bail agreement. Just shut up for a minute, and I'll tell you why I called."

He said nothing.

"Angie was killed late Wednesday night."

"What? What happened? You think I—?"

He sounded shocked. I wondered if that was a genuine response or just a good act.

"I said, shut up. No, I don't think you did it, but Knox County does. You're their number-one suspect, especially since you're conspicuously absent from home. I'll make a suggestion. You either take it, or I'll

48

report the bail violation. Then you'll lose your cash, and the cops in Ohio and Kentucky will hound your mom and sister until they find your ass."

"Okay, okay, I'm sorry. I can't believe this. What happened? What do you want?"

He lost the attitude.

"It should take you four hours to get back here," I said. "I'll give you five. If you don't check in at Prospect PD this afternoon, I'll give a Knox County dick named Hatmaker and Lieutenant Sturgill from your rat-squad all the info I've got on you, and they can pursue you as a murder suspect. Do this my way, and the worst you have to do is explain to them why you jumped bail."

He waited a few moments to speak. "Hey, I planned on showing up in court. I didn't jump bail."

"Goddamnit, Howie!"

"Okay, I'll be there."

"Where were you between 10 p.m. Wednesday and 1 a.m. Thursday morning?" I asked.

"I got here about 2 o'clock Wednesday afternoon, and I've been here ever since."

"Can anyone other than your mother verify that?"

"Yeah, her neighbor, Mrs. Baumgarten and the postman, Mr. Zuper. They've known me for years."

"With your lousy personality, I figure if you wanted Angie dead, you wouldn't hire someone, you'd want her to see you do it."

"You're wrong about that, you know. You're wrong about me. I loved her. I still do. I just hate it when I think about her with another guy." He didn't sound overly distraught.

"That's very romantic, but let me make an additional point. If you run or you've lied to me, the country is not big enough, nor are you smart enough for me not to find you. I'm not your typical jerkwater farm-cop as you called me."

"I guess I should apologize for that."

"Yes, you should, and don't forget you called me an asshole."

"Yeah, I know. You're right. I'm sorry. It won't happen again."

"Okay, apology accepted," I said. "But I need you to remember something in case you decide to thumb your nose at the favor I'm doing you. Think back to your academy class on the use of deadly force. You go on the run as a murderer and I can shoot you when you resist my arrest, which you no doubt would. Read between the lines, sport. And don't think I wouldn't like to punch your ticket for pissing me off. Do we understand each other?"

"Yeah, yeah, I hear you. Don't get excited. Look, I don't know why you're doin' this, but thanks. And like I said, I'm sorry if I acted like an asshole. I mean that."

"Okay, great. When you get back, we'll be good buddies and sit around a campfire singing *Cum By Ah.* Remember to be here by four o'clock."

"I will," he said. "But tell me what happened to Angie, please."

After giving out just enough information to satisfy Wetzel, I hung up, called Windy Hatmaker, and told him what I learned and about my theory.

"You know who drove unit 721 on the Wednesday swing shift?" I asked.

"Shore, I done got all that memorized. Ha, must be gittin' old, I jest forgot. Course I don't know. But I'll find out," he said.

"Do your guys keep their cars with them all the time?"

"Yep, they shore do. Jest one o' the perks o' the job. They give us a car ta use 'cause they pay us peanuts. No big salaries here like you guys git up in New York."

"Is that the green-eyed monster speaking to me?"

"I ain't got no green eyes, but I heard of your old department, and I'd be happy with half o' what you git."

"*They* get. I work for Prospect PD now."

"Yeah, you probably git more in ya pension than I make here."

He was correct, but he'd never hear that from me.

"Let's get back to unit 721, shall we?"

He laughed. "I'll call ya back."

It only took him ten minutes to learn that Curtis Fouts drove 721. Fouts was due in again that afternoon for another three-to-eleven tour. We planned to meet him after roll call.

I arrived at 2:30, found Hatmaker in the detective's squad room and made our way to the roll-call area. The lieutenant in charge got right down to business, and the troops were heading to their cars by 3:10. Windy happily let me take the lead.

"Officer Fouts, you remember me?" I asked.

He nodded.

"And I'm sure you know this guy here." I pointed a thumb at Windy. "We need to speak with you. Let's find a quiet spot and have a chat."

"'Bout what?" Fouts asked.

"I'll tell you when we get there."

We found the juvenile interrogation room empty and used it. Inside, Windy took out his pack of cigarettes, patted his pockets looking for a light and then asked Fouts if he had a match. Fouts took the bait and pulled a book from his shirt pocket—a matchbook from the same restaurant advertised on the matches I found on Angie's deck.

After Fouts did his one-handed match act, I took out the book I had in my jacket pocket.

"I've got one of those, too, Curt," I said, dangling the little clear plastic bag so he could see it.

He looked at me and finally remembered to blow out the match before he set his hand on fire.

"Know where I found this book of matches?" I asked.

He shook his head. "How could I?"

"On Angie Valle's deck—day after she died."

"So?"

"So, the matches are bent, just like those in your book."

"Lotta people light matches like me."

"No, they don't. And a lot of people don't leave your thumb print on the shiny cover."

I lied about that, but he didn't know it. His face dropped.

"And a lot of people don't drive car 721 and park it in front of Angie Valle's apartment after they get off work on a Wednesday evening."

"You're crazy. I didn't do nuthin' like what ya said."

"Yes, you did. Look, Angie was a good-looking girl—the right age, smart, had a good job. Her ex smacked her around a lot, too. She needed a lady's man like you to make her feel safe and better. And you wanted a new piece o' tail."

Fouts began his innocent act. He looked over at Hatmaker and made a face. Then he looked back at me.

"You got off work after her old man just threatened her," I said. "You stopped to see her—see if she was alright and if you couldn't do something for her—something in the area of love and affection."

Fouts smirked and shook his head.

"Only your standard line of bullshit didn't work. She rejected you. You didn't like that. You figured she said no, but she really meant yes. So you got a little physical. You figured these women who married tough-guys like to get roughed-up a little to get them in the mood."

Fonts subjected us to more faces. He tried to appear as if he'd suffer through my explanation, but he didn't buy it for a minute.

"But she got a little physical, too—she hit you," I continued my own act. "No reason to take that from a little girl, huh? So you smacked her—hard. You didn't mean to hurt her, just wanted to show her who's boss. How am I doing so far?"

He looked over at Hatmaker again. "Windy, who the hell's this guy, an' whatcha doin' lettin' him come in here and push his way around our case?"

"He's got some good points, Curtis," Windy said. "Cain't deny it. You are a notorious swordsman."

"Look," I said, "we're just three cops here. I don't have to tell you, this is your golden opportunity—you know that. This is a chance to tell your story. Tell us that you're not a bad guy. You're just a victim of circumstance. You didn't want that to happen. You hit her a little too hard, that's all. It was just an accident. After you hit her, you got so upset you had to go out on the deck, have a smoke, calm down and get your head straight. You felt terrible."

Fouts' face blanched. He lost the smirk and stared at me. He no longer shook his head.

"But accidents like that happen, Curtis. Probably not your fault. You know that, I know it, and Windy here knows it. Get out in front of this, and make it work for you. Make sure you're the one in control of this situation."

"Windy, you think I oughta get me a lawyer?" Fouts asked.

I didn't let Windy respond. I had Fouts thinking, and I was on a roll.

"You're going to need a good lawyer. But later, to get one of those sweetheart deals from the DA," I said. "Hey, you've been around. You know with the right attorney that can happen at the snap of your fingers."

Fouts' eyes blinked a mile a minute.

"But you lawyer-up now and I'll make sure this goes to one of those rats from Internal Affairs—a guy who isn't a street-cop like one of us. Time to keep it in the family, Curt. Keep it with the guys who understand how a woman can drive you crazy and make you so mad you just have to smack her. Remember your penal law classes, partner—no intent, no murder. No murder, no possible death penalty."

Fouts sat down at the small metal desk in the juvenile room and with shaking hands lit up a cigarette. I already had a headache from the smoke Windy puffed into the tight cramped quarters. I could have smacked both of them.

"You ain't sayin' much, Windy." Fouts sounded worried.

"He's jest about said it all, Curt. Seems these ex-New York cops can get kinda long-winded, cain't they? Look, Curtis, I'll he'p ya through this," Windy offered. "Write up whatcha did, and we'll gitcha a lawyer and a DA down here ta talk it over."

"Ya ain't gonna charge me with murder, are ya?" Fouts was grasping at straws.

"I ain't no lawyer, Curtis, but I'd guess they might could fit in a reckless or negligent manslaughter if ya laid yer cards on the table and cooperated. Manslaughter's a lot easier ta live with."

"Jesus, Windy, shouldn't I get me a lawyer before I write the statement?"

"Do the statement first," I said. "Your thoughts are fresh. Get them on paper so you can control what happens to you. Let everyone know why you did what you did. That's important. We all know lawyers usually screw up things cops can do better."

Fouts nodded. I had him.

"I gotta go out an' tell the loo-tenant what's happenin'," Windy said.

"I'll do that," I told him and dropped a legal pad on the desktop. "You hang in here, and help Curtis. Have another smoke while you're at it."

* * * *

That evening Kate and I waited for a pan of eggplant parmigiana baking in the oven. I drank a vodka gimlet, and she had a glass of imported Montepulciano.

"It never ceases to amaze me," I said. "Even mediocre cops can get a confession out of a suspect with some simple tricks. When a cop's the suspect, he falls prey to the same tricks he uses himself. You'd think they'd know better."

"Do you think he meant to kill her?" Kate asked.

"He probably didn't contemplate it before he got there. I guess he just started out wanting to get into her pants. When she said no and looked like she meant it, he got pissed. Maybe at some point he wanted to hurt her. Maybe not. Maybe it was just an accident. If he didn't confess, we had little evidence that would have convicted him. But who cares? It's not my case anymore."

"And how about the ex-husband? What do you think will happen to him?"

"If his boss has any brains, he'll fire him. The Knox County cops watching his trailer were called off when Fouts signed his confession. They don't care about him any longer. He did report in to Prospect and will probably stay put until there's either a trial or a deal is made. He's another one I can't worry about."

A buzzer sounded.

"I think our dinner is ready," Kate said.

"Good, I'm hungry."

"You're always hungry, sweetie."

* * * *

On Monday, Angie's funeral took place in North Knoxville. Her parents and a few family members flew in from her hometown of Providence to attend. The people at the TV station had taken care of the arrangements.

I stood a few yards back from the grave. Dozens of co-workers attended and listened to a priest conduct the service.

When it broke up, Rachel saw me and walked over.

"Hi, it was nice of you to come," she said. "We're all grateful you solved the case so quickly. You're a good cop."

"Aw shucks, ma'am. T'weren't nuthin'."

"Yes, it was. Thank you." She kissed my cheek.

I nodded and tried to look humble. That's usually difficult for me.

"The station manager arranged a memorial lunch for the family and all of us. Would you like to come?"

"Thanks, but I don't think so. I'm never comfortable at weddings, funerals, or Bar Mitzvahs."

She smiled.

"I really want to make an appearance and speak to her family, but if you can wait, we could go somewhere and have lunch together," she suggested.

"That's nice, but it's probably not a good idea. Not today."

"I guess."

"Another time," I said.

"Okay. You're right."

I nodded. "The world must be in bad shape if I end up being the voice of reason."

She smiled. "That's not true. You're my hero."

"Wow! I'm gonna blush."

"Let's not wait too long. I'll miss you."

"Remember the old proverb, 'Absence makes the heart grow fonder.'"

She nodded and smiled.

"Well, a wise man once said, 'Proximity makes the pants grow hotter.'"

She laughed. "I think it was a wise guy and not a wise man who said that."

"Maybe."

"I guess you have to go back to work right now?"

Prompted by the memory of something Dashiell Hammett wrote, and the movie Humphrey Bogart starred in, I stretched my lips over my teeth and said, "There's no place in this town for a shamus like me, angel. I'm goin' back to Prospect where there's danger in every back alley and trouble on every street corner."

"Trouble on every street?" She showed noticeable skepticism.

"Trouble is my middle name, doll face."

"Trouble is on your birth certificate?"

She was a tough nut to crack.

"A dame like you can be too smart for her own good."

"Is that so?" She laughed again. I love her laugh.

"If you weren't so damn good-lookin', I'd charge you twenty-five-bucks a day plus expenses."

"Okay, Bogey, I'll consider myself lucky and see you around."

I pointed at her with my index finger and let my thumb fall like the hammer of a gun.

"Yeah, see ya, sweetheart."

THE END

Bullets Off-Broadway

Wayne Zurl

Bullets Off-Broadway
Wayne Zurl

She had a black and blue mouse under her left eye and the beginnings of a cauliflower ear—not things you expect to see on a fifty-year-old woman with plenty of money.

She sat on the exam table, a doctor to her left and a nurse on her right. Sergeant Stan Rose stood next to me, ten feet from that small corner of the emergency room.

"I doubt you have a concussion," the doctor said, "but it would be best if you stayed the night."

The patient shook her head gingerly.

"Okay, but you should see your family doctor tomorrow."

The woman said nothing. The doctor understood; he'd seen her and others like her before.

"Or if you have problems, come back, and see us," he offered. "Sign the papers for Teresa, and you're free to go." He smiled and walked away.

The nurse began her explanation as if it had been recorded. I thought of the dolls my sister owned years ago. Pull the ring on their neck and listen to a recorded message. Maybe graduates had rings installed as they left nursing school.

Ella Mae Swope slowly slid off the exam table, grimaced at a stabbing pain in her side and took a moment to steady herself. She turned around and signed three hospital forms while resting the clipboard on the table's surface. The nurse swept the privacy curtain back against the wall, and Ella Mae started her walk to the lobby.

"Ella, we need to talk," I said.

"I'm really not in the mood, Chief."

"I won't keep you long, and I have to insist."

She nodded.

I looked at my watch—quarter-to-midnight. I looked at Stanley. "Go ahead, and close up shop. I'll see you tomorrow."

He nodded and left.

"The waiting room is crowded," I said, "Let's walk down the hall to the coffee shop."

Mrs. Swope followed me, declined my offer to buy her coffee and chose a table away from the half dozen other patrons scattered around the room.

I assumed Ella had once been an attractive woman. Actually, she still was until you saw the pain and hopelessness behind her outward appearance. Too many years of getting tuned up and the stress of living with a violent man hardened a once pretty face. The extra few pounds she wore probably came from no longer caring or from a few too many alcoholic calories each day. Her medium-length brown hair needed a combing as we sat at a small round table in the hospital coffee shop.

"Are you going to sign the assault complaint this time?" I asked.

"What's the use? Nothing will happen to him. Nothing will change. You won't do a damn thing yourself." She ran a hand through her hair, messing it up a little more.

"Ella, I could jump up and down on this table telling you that's not true, and you wouldn't believe me. I'll just say this once—I will do something, but you have to sign the complaint and follow through by going to court."

"What's the use?"

"What's the sense of being used as a punching bag every time Danny has a bad day?"

"He's not a bad guy. It's only when he has trouble at the yard or when he's been drinking."

"How many times has he smacked the crap out of you? How many black eyes, bruised ribs or other physical damage do you have to suffer before it sinks in that getting beaten is not part of a good marriage?"

"I know you're right. It's just—"

"Stop." I held up a hand to squelch her rationalization. "Your excuses may work on you, but not on me. Bottom line, Ella—come into the PD tomorrow, and we'll do the paperwork. Or not—your choice."

"All right, I'll sign. But are you really going to lock up a member of the city council?"

"I haven't had to before, but sure, why not? Danny needs some quality time with a good shrink. If a court order is the only way to get him there, so be it."

"You're a city employee, Sam. They'll make your life miserable."

"I'm the cop. It's my job to make people miserable. Politicians are pussycats. Besides, that's my problem.

"Now for tonight," I said, "where can I take you: mother, daughter or sister's?"

"My sister's, please."

* * * *

The chief assistant district attorney told me I was nuts. I often annoy her. Moira Menzies lectured me on the trouble I might encounter in prosecuting a local politician for domestic violence. An accurate assessment, of course. Only I didn't much care.

Later that morning, I picked up my assault warrant at the Blount County Justice Center. I received a few more bits of similar advice from the judge, all designed to make my professional life easier, but ever since I was a kid, I had this thing about seeing justice done. It's just what cowboys do.

Ella Mae's husband, Danny, owned Swope Lumber and Supply in Prospect, Tennessee, a pretty little town in the foothills of the Great Smoky Mountains.

In no way a self-made man, Danny inherited the business from his father, who in turn inherited it from his father, who founded the business in 1930-something.

For the several years I knew Danny Swope, I recognized him as a spoiled fifty-something-year-old child who drove a big Cadillac Escalade and constantly spoke of his hunting adventures. Danny had never bothered me personally, but I still didn't like his act.

"You believe that whoaman, Sam?" Danny asked. "You believe I hit her? I thought you knew your job. I'm disappointed in you, Sam. She had too much ta drink and tripped on the cellar stairs is all."

Danny thought his clever ploy of making me doubt myself would work.

"I know the difference between bruises from a fall and the marks of a good beating, Dan, and I don't much give a rat's ass what your opinion of me is."

"You callin' me a liar?

I guess he wanted to play chicken.

"If you persist in telling me you haven't beaten your wife, then you're a lying sack of shit. Clear enough?"

"Well, I'll tell you this, Mister Sam, Po-leece Chief, Jinkins, you ain't lockin' me up, nosir."

"Danny, keep your mouth shut, and listen carefully. I came in here as a courtesy to you in deference to your position in the community. I could have sent two cops and had them drag your ass out in cuffs. But no, I told you to get with your lawyer and come into my office this afternoon or tomorrow morning and surrender yourself. I'll make you that offer once more, but if you piss me off again, I'll cuff you myself and arrest you right now—in front of all your employees. Understand?" I stood up and glared at him.

He came around from behind his desk. I didn't like how fast he moved and poised to hit him. But he stopped about three feet from me, and he began to percolate.

Danny was not a tall man, only about five-foot-seven or eight, but he was built like a fire-plug. He had broad shoulders and thick arms. His wide ruddy face turned even redder with anger.

"Careful, Danny. Looks like your blood pressure is on the rise."

"Careful yerse'f, Jinkins. Last time I looked, I's one o' your bosses. Push me, an' I'll make life miserable fer ya."

I laughed, not because I found what he said humorous, but because I thought it would anger him more. If he had a stroke right there in his office, my troubles might be over.

"I'm my own boss, Danny, but I might admit to working in the best interest of the people."

He snorted and put his hands defiantly on his hips.

"Last time I looked, I'm the cop, and I can take away your freedom. You own a lumber yard. The best you can do is sell me a two-by-four.

Don't act tough with me."

I think that one got to him. He stood there seething, his jaw muscles working overtime.

"Alright, y'all will hear from my lawyer."

"Thank you, sir. Nice doing business with you."

That was how my Monday ended.

* * * *

The kid's Model 19 barked six times. He opened the cylinder, ejected the spent shells and reloaded using a speed-loader. He fired six more rounds. We walked seven yards to the target-line for a look.

"Not bad, Junior," I said. "Only three nines, the rest 10s and Xs. I guess you killed him."

"Shoot, Sam, I thought I might o' cleaned this one."

The kid stood as tall as me—six foot—but had me by a solid twenty pounds. He had just gotten a haircut—almost a crew cut. Junior Huskey was a good-looking boy and a good cop.

"You get this double action shooting down pat," I said, "and shooting with your Glock will be a piece of cake."

"Yeah, I know."

"Let's go back to fifteen yards and see what happens," I suggested.

I fired six rounds, reloaded and fired six more.

"One more look," I said.

We walked back to the target-line.

"Gat dag," the kid said. "Ya cleaned it. Good shootin', boss."

There were nine Xs and three 10s—one straddling the 9 ring.

"Look at that flyer on the 9 ring. I'm shootin' like an old lady."

My cell phone rang. Junior had shown me how to download a music ring-tone. The Rolling Stones played *Paint it Black*.

"Hello, Sammy, you and Junior doin' all right today?"

"Hi ya, Betts," I said to Sergeant Bettye Lambert. "You checking up on me?"

"I hate to bother you at the range, darlin', but you need to drive back here."

I didn't give her a chance to explain before I asked, "What's up? I was just about to whip the kid's backside at twenty-five yards."

"I know you two are havin' fun, but one of the good folks of Prospect's gotten themselves killed."

* * * *

Bettye's comment about the victim being one of the good folks of Prospect was an overstatement. The deceased was Danny Swope, not one of my favorite people on that Wednesday morning.

I walked up next to PO Lenny Alcock who stood watching two county crime scene investigators and one of our medical examiners and his assistant process the murder scene and deal with the victim. I put my hand on Alcock's shoulder.

"What do you know, Lenny?"

"Hey, boss, you doin' aw rot today?"

"Better than him," I pointed at Danny Swope.

"Shot twice. That's all I know so far."

We stood in the yard of Swope Lumber, next to an outdoor storage shed full of treated two-bys. Danny lay face up. A pool of blood created a wide circle beneath and around him.

"Hi ya, Mo," I said to Dr. Morris Rappaport. "Know anything worth hearing yet?"

"Samilah, you always ask me for an opinion before I can give one. Have patience, young man. Have patience."

"Morris, I'm older than you." Mo was in his mid-fifties. "I may not have that much time left. Besides, I was born impatient. Even something small would be a help."

"Well, he's dead."

"Oy, I think your parents wasted their hard-earned money on tuition. I can see he's dead from here, and I'm not the fakocktah doctah."

Morris was a nice Jewish boy from New Jersey.

"We've just started. He was shot twice, I can tell you."

"If I put on my glasses I could see that, too. Shot with what? Bullets? An arrow? A spear gun?"

"Two big holes, Sam. I'm guessing a .45."

"Ouch."

"Yes, ouch. Now can I get back to work?"

"Of course. Pretend I'm not here."

"Did you bother the MEs this much when you worked in New York?"

"Who me?" I smiled for Morris and spoke to his assistant, Earl Ogle. "Keep an eye on him, Earl. Make sure he doesn't lose my bullets."

"I'll do the best I kin, but ya know how the good doctor here is set in his ways."

I took a few steps to where the two evidence technicians, Jackie Shuman and David Sparks, looked for clues.

"See any hot prospects for evidence, gents?"

"Hey, Sam," Jackie said. "I'd love ta tell ya yes, but they's a million footprints and tire tracks criss-crossed all over here and there. Ain't found no shell casins yet, so either he's shot with a revolver or the shooter picked up his brass."

That didn't sound encouraging.

"You have anything to say, young Sparks?" I asked David.

"Hey, Chief, you doin' aw rot today?" He spoke in the soft accent of the people who've lived in the mountains for generations.

* * * *

Mayor Ronnie Shield's office looks like the waiting room at a rod and gun club. I sat in a dark green leather chair facing his desk. The sad eyes of a ten-point buck looked down at me. The glazed, yellow eyes of a great northern pike looked at me, too; its toothy snarl seemed malevolent. From framed prints hanging all over the walls, more white-tail deer, wild turkeys, black bear and large-mouth bass looked at me from various angles.

Ronnie Shields looked out of his bay window at the town square rather than at me.

"Lord have mercy, Sam. Why'd ya go and git an arrest warrant fer Danny?"

Ronnie looked much younger than his forty-six years. He had one of those perpetual little-boy faces.

"Because he beat the shit out of his wife. They wanted to admit her to the hospital, but she refused. And this was only the most recent occurrence."

"He was a city councilman, Sam. Couldn't ya have done it some other way?"

I think Ronnie knew he'd get nowhere with me, but he tried anyway.

"Danny had many opportunities to get help with his abuse problems. He never did. He never even acknowledged having a problem. This was the first time Ella Mae signed a complaint."

"And now y'all have ta arrest her fer his murder."

"I don't know that Ella killed him. I only left the crime scene," I looked at my watch, "a little over an hour ago."

"Well, who do ya think killed him then?" Ronnie gets exasperated easily.

"Who knows? The longer I hang around here…"

"I know, I know. Lord have mercy, Sam…please keep me informed."

* * * *

It was a warm September day. The digital thermometer on the Prospect Citizen's Bank showed eighty degrees, and there wasn't a cloud in the sky. I drove into the Yorkshire Dales subdivision looking for the Swope homestead.

I took a left on Rowcliffe Road and then at the highest point in the development, a right onto Mountain View Drive. In the middle of three lots, perched on the side of a steep cliff, Danny Swope had built a three level hacienda worth a million plus.

I parked my unmarked Ford and went to knock on a front door that must have cost more than the gross national product of Andorra. Ella Mae answered. A fresh bruise showed on her cheek. It looked like Danny's Masonic ring had broken the skin.

"Ella, I'm sorry for your loss," I said, knowing she must have mixed emotions.

"Thank you. Come in, please." Her eyes were red and glassy. She had cried more than a little.

We sat in the living room. A row of five double French-doors led to a wraparound deck overlooking a valley. Several five-thousand-foot mountains stood off in the distance.

"Would you like coffee or iced tea or something?"

"No thanks, but I have to ask a few questions," I said.

"I know."

"Normally, I'd just start off and see where my questions lead me, but under the circumstances, I'm sure you can understand it would be best if I advise you of your rights and suggest you have an attorney present if you want one."

"Thank you, Sam. I know the spouse is always suspect, but I don't need a lawyer. You're the one who said I should have Danny put in jail, but I didn't shoot him. And before you ask, yes, he hit me again—last night when he came home, and I was here. You can guess he wasn't happy to hear about the complaint I signed."

"I'm sorry that happened, but it's...well, I'm sorry."

She nodded and waited for what I'd say next.

"I have to ask you questions like where were you early this morning."

"I was here. After he hit me, I slept in one of the guest rooms. I heard him get up and leave for work before seven o'clock. After that, I called my sister again. She got here just after nine and left before you arrived."

"Danny has a few guns registered to him. If they're here, I'd like to see them."

"They're in his den. Come on, we'll get them."

On the third floor, we entered a large room with a cathedral ceiling. After a quick look around, I thought thanks to Danny Swope, a neighborhood taxidermist might have sent his kids to college—free and clear.

On the walls hung a buffalo, an elk with a rack about six-foot across, several deer and antelope, two black bear, a wild boar...I could go on. Danny Swope, great white hunter.

I didn't think Danny killed all those animals with a stone and slingshot like David killed Goliath. Against the outside wall, a beautiful golden oak gun-cabinet stood with a dozen long guns inside—rifles and shotguns. Before I checked the guns in the cabinet, Ella opened a large old-fashioned gun safe for me. Inside I found nine handguns.

"There are six more pistols here than he had on paper," I said.

"I don't know anything about his guns," Ella said. "He bought some from that store in Maryville, and I guess some at gun shows. He was always going to them."

A few things on a wall rack in the corner of the room caught my eye. A big white, Montana-style Stetson hung on the end hook while a half-dozen different old west gun belts and holsters filled the remaining spots.

I walked over, Ella followed. I picked up the hat and looked inside. Embossed letters on the sweatband told me Danny's cowboy hat was made of 15X beaver felt by a company from Omaha. Looking at the gun rigs, I saw some were hand tooled; all were high quality and expensive-looking.

"Your husband liked the old west?"

"I guess he did. He was always going to those cowboy shooting matches, once a month, maybe."

"Did he belong to the club that shoots up in Oak Ridge?"

"I think so, yes."

* * * *

Back at the department, Bettye buzzed my phone.

"Earl Ogle, Doctor Mo's assistant, is on the line. He's got some information from the autopsy."

I listened as Earl relayed some specifics.

"Doc done took them two slugs outta yer victim. Says they's two one-hunnert-an'-ninety grain soft lead .45s, probably from a revolver 'cause the soft lead mighta jammed in the chamber of an automatic. I sent 'em over ta TBI ballistics for them ta git workin' on the riflin' marks. Yer boy was shot up close. One real close and one not so close. One didn't do much damage and wouldn'ta killed him, but the other got him di-rectley in the heart."

"So, what do you figure, practice loads rather than hot factory stuff?"

"Be my guess."

"Practice loads, like cowboy target shooters might use?"

"I ain't yer ballistics man, but that would be my guess."

* * * *

After some quick computer work, Bettye learned a few things about the Smoky Mountain Shootist Society, the local cowboy action-shooting group. The club's secretary, a man named Ed Smiley, lived and worked in Prospect. Lucky me.

There are advantages to being a small town cop. I knew Ed Smiley and lots of other folks in Prospect. In New York, where I used to work, I knew less than one-percent of the people they asked me to police up after.

I took a short drive to Cyber-Space Solutions, Ed Smiley's computer sales and service store.

After a quick greeting and a few exchanged pleasantries, I asked, "Where the hell'd you get a name like that for your business?"

"It's modern, up-to-date. Kinda catches the fancy of the young folks. They trust you if you're state-of-the-art."

"You're older than me. What young folks are going to trust you?"

"You come here to harass me or talk about cowboy shootin'?"

"Actually, I came to talk about murder."

Ed's big brown eyes popped wide, and his open mouth left a noticeable gap in a short gray beard.

I explained my reference to murder and asked what he knew about Danny Swope, who, I learned, shot under the registered alias of Deadwood Dan.

I couldn't help but wonder if my Smoky Mountain gunslinger had played poker that morning and drew a hand of aces and eights.

"Well, I don't want ta sound like I'm tellin' tales outta school," Smiley said, "but I guess if Danny hung out with anyone in particular, it would have been Dakota Lil."

"Tell me that's her shooting name, please."

"Well, o' course. When everybody's all dressed up in their old west clothes at the shoots, we're all called to the firing line by alias. I just mostly call everybody by their SASS names."

"SASS?"

"Single Action Shooting Society. All the clubs are affiliated with and sanctioned by SASS. They're the ones who register the aliases and make sure there's no duplications."

"Heaven forbid. Can't have two Deadwood Dan's ridin' the range. How can you protect your reputation?"

Ed frowned at my observation.

"By the way, what's your alias?" I asked.

He hesitated answering. I suppose he could foresee another smartass remark about his chosen pastime.

Then he relented. "I'm Clint Southwood."

"Uh-huh." I let the dreadfully clever idea I had about preferring to be called by the real Clint's spaghetti western handle, 'the man with no name', go by the wayside.

I refocused our conversation back to police business. "What's Lil's real name?"

"Dakota Lil is Krista Vetch," he said. "She lives in Maryville. I think she still works at the Wal-Mart down on 411."

"Why not Kansas Krista? Sounds better than Virginia Vetch which could be some kind of plant life."

"Do what?"

Ed needed to have his sense of humor checked.

* * * *

I got no answer at Krista's listed home phone. I decided to gamble—I was really getting into the old west thing—and try to find Dakota Lil working at Sam Walton's General Store.

I rode west out of Prospect and followed the settin' sun, so to speak. Actually, I took US-321 to US-411 and turned south. In twenty minutes, I pulled into the Wal-Mart lot and hitched my big dapple-gray Ford gelding to a parking spot.

After being shuffled between several underlings, I finally ended up with the trail boss...or store manager.

"Sorry," he said. "I see Ms. Vetch has taken a sick day."

"Rats!" I said—to myself—not the trail boss who was kind enough to give me her cell phone number.

That was the magic number. Krista answered—somewhere in a Food Lion parking lot. We agreed to meet at her home in thirty minutes. I got there early.

Krista wasn't exactly pretty, but she was a nice-looking woman who, at forty-four, still had a good figure. Not as good as Bettye Lambert who's the same age, or my wife, for that matter, who's older. Both those women are very pretty. But I'm wandering off the topic.

Anyway, all three would probably look great dressed as Dodge City saloon girls.

I learned that Krista had heard about Danny's murder on the morning news. She looked sad, sad enough to need a day off, but not exactly distraught.

I began my interview with a good old-fashioned lie. "I've spoken to a number of people from the SASS crowd, both locally and where you two went to shoot, and several people told me that you and Danny were an item."

Surprisingly, that took her back. She denied any romantic involvement—vehemently. Sure I had guessed correctly, I just needed her to admit it.

"If I've gotten to you this easily in such a short time, don't you think in another day or so I'll be able to put you two together in a motel or bedroom somewhere?"

She looked at me for a long moment. It was difficult for me to believe, but her expression didn't indicate that I was one of her favorite people at the moment. Finally, she thought honesty might be the best policy.

"Danny's marriage was over," she said. "He told me he was going to divorce his wife. He only had to get some legal things taken care of so *she* couldn't get hold of his business."

Another thing that's hard to believe: Some women still fall for that old 'get some legal business finished first' ploy.

"You should know how long things take in court," she said.

I nodded. I can be very understanding at times.

"When that was finished," she said, "and *she* was out of the house, we were going to get together. When his divorce came through, we were getting married."

Sure, I thought, and you'd ride off into the sunset on Trigger and Buttermilk. Well, *she* sounded convinced.

"So you guys were just having a simple affair?" I asked.

"Yes, I guess you could say that."

"Look, Krista, I'm about the least judgmental guy you'll ever meet." Some people might say that was another lie. "I won't criticize two people who meet and fall in love, especially under those circumstances. But I've got to ask you a couple of questions that may sound intrusive."

She nodded.

"The easy one is about Danny. Now that he's dead this can't hurt him any longer." I paused to let her think about that. "Several people have told me about Danny's problem of—what should I call it—anger management?" She nodded again. "I don't know if you're aware of it, but Danny had been beating his wife for a long time. That's something for me to look at and consider—for her sake, maybe. Did Danny ever get violent with you?"

"With me?"

She answered too quickly. And she answered a question with a question. Not good.

"Yes, did he ever threaten you or hit you?"

"Me? Why would he?"

More questions.

"I spent a lot of time at your job before I came here." *I am such a liar.* "And some of the workers there say you've come to work with bruises." *Gambling and bluffing—every cowboy should know how.*

"Who told you that?"

"People. You think if I went to Blount Memorial Hospital and looked for your name in their ER files or contacted your medical insurance company I'd get lucky?"

"Why are you asking me these things? Do you think I killed Danny?"

"I'm a cop. I get paid to ask questions. I expect honest answers. They make me think you're innocent."

She repositioned herself on the chair and waited a long moment before answering. "Well, maybe he did hit me—once or twice. Danny had a lot of pressure from his wife and at his job. He was an important man, you know, in the City Council and all."

"Okay, here's the tough question, Krista. Did you kill Danny?"

"Lord have mercy, no!"

"He was killed by two rounds of .45 Long Colt—cowboy shooter's ammunition."

"Lotsa people shoot .45s."

"You too?"

"Me? No, I've got a pair of .38s"

If my wife or Bettye said that, I would have raised my eyebrows, given them a lecherous grin and risked getting slapped.

"I'm going to check the firearms records," I said. "Did you buy the guns legally, over-the-counter somewhere?"

She crossed her arms defensively over her breasts. "I surely did."

"Do you have any other handguns or a rifle that shoots .45s?"

It's difficult to describe her expression other than indignant. "No, sir, I do not."

"Can I see your guns? Just to verify they're not .45s?"

She disappeared for a couple of minutes and returned carrying a pair of shiny, stainless steel .357 magnum Ruger Vaqueros with faux pearl grips. Both guns fired .38 Special ammunition. The pair was housed in dark russet holsters, decorated by silver conchas.

"Does every shooter use two guns?"

"We use four."

"Four? Where do you put them all?"

She wrinkled up her face, indicating I was frightfully uneducated in the world of SASS.

"Two pistols, a rifle and a shotgun," she said.

"You shoot a rifle and a shotgun, too?"

She nodded.

"I'm impressed."

She smiled.

"Can I see those?"

She got them, a replica of an 1892 Winchester carbine also chambered for .357 and a double-barreled .20 gauge coach gun.

I'll remember not to mess with Dakota Lil.

* * * *

If someone pressed me for an opinion, I'd say Krista probably didn't kill Danny Swope. But I'd look further and still keep her on the back burner or maybe the tailgate of the chuck wagon.

When I walked back into the office, I found Jackie Shuman talking with Bettye.

"Here's yer reports, pitchers and gun inventory, boss-man," he said.

I pulled all the paperwork out of the nine-by-twelve envelope he handed me.

"You're a fine American, young feller. Find anything that'll help me solve this case?"

"Sorry 'bout that. Not a gat-dag thing. 'Cuse me, Miss Bettye."

Miss Bettye smiled graciously.

"No forensics, huh? Then good old-fashioned police work is all I've got?"

"'Fraid so. Sorry I cain't he'p ya more."

"Never fear, old chap," I said with a pompous British accent, "but the game's afoot, and I shall persevere with great vigor. Ha, ha!"

"Sammy," Bettye said, "y'all can be so funny at times."

I may have amused Sergeant Lambert, but I really didn't know diddly-squat about who killed Danny Swope. I had spent a day plodding around and so far had nothing. I was hungry, tired, and I wanted to go home. I'd look for inspiration…and a drink…from my wife and dog.

* * * *

I started the next morning by looking over the crime scene photos and sketch. I read the reports, all of which told me nothing more than I already knew. Then, for lack of anything else to do, I looked over the inventory of Danny's firearms.

After only a minute of reading, I noticed something was missing. Discounting the modern sporting guns, I saw listed an Italian-made replica of an 1873 Winchester rifle chambered in .45 Long Colt caliber, a .12 gauge shotgun and a .45 caliber Colt single action Army revolver with a five-and-one-half-inch barrel. Only one .45 caliber revolver. I remembered back to Krista's comment, 'We all shoot four guns.' One of Danny's pistols had gone missing.

I called Bill Werner, the firearms examiner at the Tennessee Bureau of Investigation in Knoxville.

"You know anything more about those .45 slugs that came out of my victim?"

"I've just finished the work on them," he said. "I'm thinking they have to be from a Colt single action, probably one with a five-and-a-half-inch barrel. I'd testify to that. Don't think they were fired from one of the imported replicas."

Bill, another transplanted northerner, spent all his days testing firearms for the cops in Tennessee.

"Willy, I'm glad you said that. You give credence to a theory I'm formulating."

"Happy to help, Sam. If I can do anything—"

"Whoa, podna." The cowboy thing had really taken hold of me. "I believe my vic was shot with his own gun, and I'm thinking that gun is missing from his collection.

"Jackie Shuman brought you a whole mess of guns from the victim, Danny Swope. One of those on the inventory is a third generation Colt single action with a five-and-a-half-inch barrel."

"Well now," he said.

"Well now, indeed. How about you test that Colt for me, and either tell me it's similar to the murder weapon, or it's the one that killed poor old Dakota Dan."

"Who?"

"Don't ask."

"I've got a few things on my list that have priority over test-firing an inventory of guns, you know."

"Bill, old buddy, I'd sure appreciate you moving that one gun up to the top of your list."

"You know, Sam, I've heard that you've been seen more than once having lunch at Chesapeake's."

I knew where the conversation was heading.

"Tell you what, old buddy," he said. "For an invitation to lunch at Chesapeake's, I might just be able to squeeze in that test today."

Bill's heart was as cold as his Michigan roots.

"Deal," I said. "Call me as soon as you finish. And it's lunch, not dinner. Those bastards are too expensive at night."

"Lunch it is. I'll call you later."

I really need an expense account.

* * * *

Later that day, Bill Werner told me two things. The gun he tested was not the murder weapon, but it was probably a very close family member to the gun that did kill Danny Swope.

A search for the missing Colt in Danny's office at the lumberyard and in his gaudy black Escalade, still parked there, netted me nothing.

On the way back to the PD, I passed the city park. For no particular reason I drove up McTeer's Station Road toward the reconstructed 18th century settler's fort. I go there occasionally to commune with history or think about a case. It's a quiet and peaceful spot.

I parked the Crown Vic and walked through the sally port of the tall stockade wall. Off to my left stood a two-story blockhouse. To the right, Robert McTeer's log cabin. And strung along the palisades were slant-roofed structures: storage sheds, guest accommodations and animal shelters.

It was early autumn and still warm, both during the day and through the night. I shouldn't have smelled the remnants of a wood fire, but I did.

I walked over toward the log cabin. As I approached slowly, I felt a wave of pricklies travel up my spine. I knew I wasn't alone. The feeling was familiar, from my time as a soldier and from my time as a uniformed cop walking the streets on a midnight tour. Someone else was there, somewhere close.

I picked a blind spot in the cabin wall, a spot nowhere near a window, and hopped up to the raised wooden porch. The rubber soles of my L.L. Bean boat shoes allowed me to do that silently. I stopped, listened and sniffed. Had I done that in Vietnam I might have smelled body odor or nuoc mam, the salty fish sauce that lingered on people's breath forever. On that day, I smelled wood smoke, unpainted lumber and perspiration.

I drew my old Smith and Wesson, got a tight grip with both hands and moved slowly toward the cabin door. If no one was present I'd feel foolish, but who would care? If someone was there, he was mine, and I'd care.

Two feet from the door, I stopped and listened again. A slight breeze rustled in the trees. Birds chirped and flitted from branch to branch, barely audible unless I strained my ears. A squirrel chattered to a mate or to no one in particular. My breathing was shallow. I could hear my heart beat. I heard someone or something breathing, living, inside the cabin.

They tried to be quiet, but I could hear them.

I waited silently and made a plan. I'd push open the cabin door. It opened on my right. I'd have a clear view to the whole right side of the one-room cabin, the fireplace side of the room. If necessary, I'd enter the cabin to see what lay to the left. If the person there had any skills or intelligence, he'd move to the left corner near the door—the place I'd see last.

Cops and private eyes on television jump into a room, exposing themselves to possible gunfire and yell 'freeze', like that would have some influence on a subject waiting for them. No real cop would or should ever do that.

I pushed the door open slowly and saw a clear room to the right. Only half the job was done. By quickly bobbing my head in and out of the cabin, I saw no one in the far left corner of the room. Only one place remained. I took a breath, mustered up a little more moxey and stuck my head in and out once again—quickly—looking to the near left corner.

Someone sat huddled in that corner.

"I'm a police officer," I said. "I'm holding a gun. Move to the center of the room."

I heard nothing.

"Move, goddamnit! Move now, or I'll start shooting!"

I wouldn't have, of course, but it always works better if the person you're confronting thinks you're crazy.

"Okay, okay, Jesus Christ. Don't shoot. I'm only crashing here," a male voice said.

"Listen carefully." I spoke loudly. "I want you to crawl out on the floor. Let me see your hands. I'll kill you if you move too fast."

I peeked around the doorframe and made eye contact with my subject. He looked to be my age.

"Okay, brother," he said, "Be cool. Chieu hoi. Chieu hoi."

'Chieu hoi?' I thought back forty years, and another chill ran up my spine. I'd heard that one before, and I didn't trust it any more now than I did then. I yelled out a command I had used before, something I heard said by more GIs than I could accurately count, "Dung lai, motherfucker! On your belly—now!"

"Jesus, man. Be cool. Be cool. This ain't the Nam. Just be cool."

"I hear you. Make your move now. Slowly."

I heard, and then I saw a body low-crawl into the center of the room.

"I'm here, man. Don't fuckin' shoot me," he said, "I'm one of the good guys."

A shabbily dressed man lay spread-eagle on the rough wooden floor of the cabin. I moved in holding my gun on him, approaching him from his blind side.

"Don't move. Not even an inch." I patted him down for a weapon.

"I'm not armed," he said. "I've got a knife in my rucksack, but I've got nothing on me."

I sat down on the floor and realized that my prisoner didn't look like a significant threat. Perhaps I over-reacted. I let out a big breath. "Son-of-a-bitch. Man, you damn sure got my adrenaline flowing."

"Sorry, brother," he said. "I mean no harm. I'm just looking for a dry spot to make lunch."

I looked again at the prostrate figure on the floor. Faded blue jeans, an old Army field jacket when it was too warm to need one, gray hair too long for the current style, and a face long overdue for a shave.

"Sit up." I said. "Sorry to put you through all this, but…but maybe you know how it is. Relax. I'm a cop."

"I'm gettin' up now, slowly. Okay?"

"Yeah, get up. Everything's cool."

"Jesus, man. I ain't never seen anybody do that any better. You had me shittin' in my pants."

"I've had a little practice."

"I guess."

"Who are you?" I asked.

"Name's Bobby Foster. I'm just passing through. Don't mean nobody no harm—honest."

"I'm Sam Jenkins, Bobby. I mean no harm either."

'Chieu hoi', in Vietnamese, literally means open arms or figuratively, I surrender. Something a Viet Cong sapper might say before walking into a group of waiting GIs while carrying a satchel charge of explosives. I don't think I would have fired on Bobby Foster unless I saw a weapon, but I know that expression saved his life. 'Dung lai' is the command to give up and obey. That other phrase was only me lapsing into my potty-mouth ways of years ago.

We sat on the floor and talked for a few minutes.

"So where were you?" I asked. "Who were you with?" Two vague questions, maybe, but he knew exactly what I meant.

"Charley Company, 1st of the 199th Light Infantry, whole time."

"I remember you guys from Bien Hoa and Long Binh. I was at Camp Ho Gnoc Tao over in Tay Ninh."

"Sure, I know where that was, west end of Three Corps," he said.

"What are you doing in beautiful downtown Prospect?"

"Just kinda hangin' out. As you can see, life ain't been so good to me. I'm not a prosperous middle-aged gentleman like you."

"When did you eat last?"

"I had something this morning. I'm doing okay."

"You want some lunch? I'm hungry, and I'm buying."

"Shit, brother, I won't say no."

We drove to Howell's Pub where Bobby's appearance wouldn't look too much out of place.

We arrived at 12:30 and didn't find as much of a crowd as usual. Reggie, the manager and bartender, came over, said hello and asked what we wanted. Bobby asked for a Budweiser. I chose a black and tan, a fifty-fifty mix of Guinness stout and Bass ale.

We both ordered barbeque pork sandwiches with side dishes of cole slaw and baked beans. We talked some more.

"You're not a local," he said.

"No, I'm from New York. How about you?"

"Indiana. Here and there in Indiana, but Fort Wayne originally. I like it down here in the mountains."

"You and the other half of the mid-west. I retired here and then took this police job a couple years ago."

"You a cop in New York?"

"Yeah, for twenty years on Long Island."

"Seen your share?"

"Here and there."

"I hear ya."

"I hate to say this, Bobby, but if you're hanging around here for a while you can't live in that cabin in the city park."

"Yeah, I figured. I'm on the way to Key West. I want to get there before the cold weather."

"Sounds like a plan."

"Yeah, I get by."

"I haven't seen you around the park before. Where have you been staying?"

"Last couple of nights I crashed in the lumber yard not far from here. It's nice and dry under those sheds that cover the lumber. Nobody sees me if I'm out before seven in the morning or so."

Son-of-a-gun.

"Were you there night before last?"

"I was." He frowned a little at that question.

"Want another beer?" I asked.

"Don't mind if I do."

Being a great detective isn't difficult if you find the right people and ask the right questions. With two new pints on the table, I began asking.

"Who and what did you see early that morning?"

"They started gettin' there early that day. I don't know, I'm guessing, quarter to seven, probably a little earlier."

"Who are they?"

"Workers I guess, maybe not. First one was a woman. Couple minutes later a big guy gets there. Guy with a shaved head and a little beard. Right after that, another guy pulls in with a big black Caddy van. They all drove vans or I guess they're really SUVs. The woman had a smaller, silver one. The bald guy drove a real big green thing."

"Okay, we've got a cast of characters. Now what happened?"

"I was already awake for a while, just hangin' out. Then the silver car came in and parked next to the shed where I was. Then the green car came in, and the big guy got into the silver car with the woman."

"What's the woman look like?"

"Not bad-lookin'. Actually, kinda nice, about fifty or so. Dark hair. Nice clothes."

"What do you remember about the vehicles?"

"The green one had a GMC logo on the back. The silver one, I don't know, but that one had a vanity plate. I remember that much."

He paused and sipped his beer. I waited.

"Kinda strange plate, all one word, ELLATWO. Couldn't figure out what it meant."

Over the years, I've had a lot of practice perfecting my poker-face. Outwardly, I wanted to appear the cool professional. After I heard about the license plate, I wanted to chug-a-lug my black and tan, jump off the bench, kick my heels together and shout zippity-doo-dah. But I continued to behave like a TV cop.

"What happened when the black Caddy pulled in?"

"He didn't park next to the other cars, but pulled over by the office. I could tell he was lookin' for the others 'cause he got right outta the Caddy. And maybe he didn't run, but he sure moved out smartly gettin' over to where the other two were parked."

After another sip of Bud, he continued.

"I figured maybe the woman was his wife and the big guy her boyfriend."

"Any particular reason you thought that?"

"Yeah, the guy from the Caddy had a gun."

Zippity-doo-dah! Hot-diggity-dog!

"Handgun? Rifle?"

"Handgun. A kinda big one."

"Then what happened?"

"The Caddy guy started yellin'. The other two got outta the silver car, and all three started arguing."

"You're doing great."

"Yeah, but I figured it was my time to get lost. I grabbed up my stuff and beat it while they were makin' noise. I didn't want to get involved." He paused again and took a long drink of his Budweiser. "I *don't* want to get involved."

"I'm afraid, Bobby, you're about as much involved now as when you got your draft notice forty years ago."

He rolled his eyes.

"I'm not going to send you on a twelve month hard-tour," I said. "But I can give you three hots and a cot while you're hanging around here waiting to give a statement and maybe testify. Cool, huh? Just like the green machine." I smiled.

"Yeah? No kiddin? You'll feed me and put me up? Where do I

sleep—in a cell?"

"I'll get you a nice motel room. No kidding."

"A motel? All right!"

Some people are easy to please.

"Good—now one last question. While you were making your tactical withdrawal, did you hear anything?"

"Yeah, and I still know the difference between a gunshot and a backfire. Two shots, big caliber—boom, boom."

* * * *

Bettye confirmed that Ella Mae Swope drove a silver Chevy Trailblazer with the Tennessee vanity plate ELLATWO. Ella was at home when I arrived on Mountain View Drive.

"Want coffee?" she asked.

"No thanks."

"How are things going with the investigation?"

"Not too bad. I found a homeless man today. I know he's got something to do with all this."

"You think he killed Danny? Have you arrested him?"

"No, I haven't arrested anyone yet."

She poured herself a glass of iced tea and added a wedge of lemon.

"Need more evidence or something?"

"I need to find out a little more about Danny's time line that morning."

She nodded.

"What time did he leave here again?" I asked.

"I'm not sure. I was still asleep. But I know it was before seven."

"What time did you wake up?"

"Around eight."

"How do you know he left before seven if you were asleep?"

"Well, ah…I just assumed."

"Okay, you're up around eight—then what?"

"I called my sister, showered, did my hair and started breakfast when Molly got here. Then you called about Danny."

"You're sure you didn't hear or see Danny leave the house?"

"No, I was asleep."

Ella will never get nominated for an Academy Award.

"Kind of difficult for someone to be in two places at one time, isn't it, Ella?"

"What do you mean?" She feigned a confused look.

"How can you be here in bed and at the lumber yard in your SUV at the same time?"

"I don't…"

I held up a hand to stop her lies.

"You know exactly what I mean. The homeless man isn't a suspect. He's my witness."

"And you're going to believe some vagrant?"

Isn't it amazing how rich people would like you to think they have more veracity than a homeless person—just because they are what they are?

"He's homeless, not an idiot, a drunk or some other kind of mindless individual. He's intelligent, and he has a good memory. And very good eyesight."

"Then you know it wasn't my fault, and I didn't shoot Danny."

She quickly changed her tune.

"Why don't you take the opportunity to fill in the blanks for me? I know what happened. You tell me why. The witness remembered your plate number. Who's the big guy with the green GMC?"

"Bo Hargis."

"Let's start at the beginning. Why were you at the lumber yard?"

"Bo had…drugs for me. When I needed them, we met there—off hours. It was safe and private. I have an automatic gate opener."

"How did you explain your absences to Danny?"

"I didn't have to. After he hit me, I would usually lock myself in a guest room. I did that night, too. The next day, I left early…about 6:30. I thought he'd assume I went to my sister's to avoid him. I was wrong. He thought I was having an affair, and I guess he followed me."

Ella Mae continued to speak of the assorted contusions and a couple of broken bones suffered at the hands of the dastardly Deadwood Dan.

I envisioned him tying the poor damsel to the railroad tracks, a la Simon Legree. But the closest tracks ran through Louisville, several miles away.

With some shame, she admitted obtaining prescription painkillers, Vicodin and others of that ilk, after each injury. The more she took, the more she needed—not necessarily for the physical pain. Things got bad when she started washing down a handful of pills with chardonnay spritzers.

Then enter Bo Hargis, friendly neighborhood pill-pusher. He was only too happy to provide Ella with her pharmaceutical needs when the licensed physicians thought it imprudent to do so.

She also admitted having a brief sexual relationship with Hargis. Not exactly romantic, but certainly physical. All that probably took place while Deadwood Dan was off popping caps and doing the horizontal square dance with Dakota Lil.

It sounded like she thought Danny was, that morning, more inclined to focus on the threat of his wife cuckolding him in the eyes of the community than worrying about her addiction to opiates. At least his last conversation with Bo and Ella centered on the former topic.

Not liking what he heard from his wife's boyfriend, Dangerous Danny drew his hog-leg and threatened Bo.

No matter what sort of pistolero badass Deadwood Dan fancied himself, he was no match for Kid Hargis, who I later learned had done some serious jail-time in both Tennessee and Alabama.

Hargis' beefy six-foot-five-inch frame presented Danny with something of a logistical problem. According to Ella, before Danny could cock the hammer of his single action revolver, Hargis grabbed hold of the barrel, wrenched the gun free and threatened to stick it where the sun didn't shine unless Danny retired to his office and allowed Bo and Ella to conclude their business.

Danny, fool that he was, tried to retrieve his peacemaker and, during a brief tussle, took one shot to his stomach. Hargis, like any no-account outlaw, knew that dead men tell no tales, so he added a second hundred-and-ninety grains of lead to Danny's heart. That ended the confrontation at Swope's Corral. Hargis kept Deadwood Dan's six-shooter, and Miss Ella jumped into her Chevy buckboard and high-tailed it outta Tombstone.

"I'll need a statement from you on all this, Ella," I said.

"Don't I need a lawyer first?"

"Although your husband was killed while you were committing a crime, it sounds like you never could have known Hargis would kill Danny. The DA may want to charge you with felony murder, but it would probably be a waste of time. So, I'll offer you a walk on the attempted purchase of the controlled substance and immunity on any murder or manslaughter charges if you make a statement. All you tell me has to prove to be true, and you have to agree to complete an accredited rehab program. That work for you?"

"You'd do that for me?"

"It's no free ride. You have to sign the statement, testify against Bo and get clean of your drug habit."

"Okay, I can do that, if I have to."

I envisioned the song and dance I'd get from Moira Menzies when she learned of my offer. Maybe I'd need drugs.

* * * *

Bo Hargis lived in the neighboring community of Rockford, at a place named by someone with a sense of humor. The Off-Broadway Trailer Park looked like anything but a local representation of one of those side streets running perpendicular to New York's Great White Way. On a gravel road running perpendicular to Broadway Avenue, an old sign marked the entrance to the trailer park. Printed in black art deco letters, it was so faded that it might have been first painted when Clarke Gable worked as a stagehand.

The Department of Motor Vehicles listed a new GMC Yukon XL registered to Robert "Bo" Hargis. The Off-Broadway community didn't look like many of its residents could afford to spend more than seventy grand on basic transportation.

I had Junior Huskey sitting with me in my unmarked Ford. Murn Ballew, the Rockford police chief and his right-hand man, Officer Cody Boone, offered us back-up. We were the posse, and we were fixin' to capture the man who gunned down Deadwood Dan.

As we drove into the trailer park, I noticed the area looked more extensive than I thought it would. Gravel roads ran off the main unnamed road that shot off Broadway. The neighborhood consisted of antique single-wides and permanently moored travel trailers. These were all placed in a semi-orderly fashion much too close for comfort. You couldn't pass gas without your neighbors commenting on your manners.

A few mangy dogs roamed the grounds, but paid us no attention. Most of the dwellings had one or two ratty vehicles parked on cracked and patched blacktop aprons set between the lots.

The place looked like a deadbeat's delight. None of the homes had numbers, and there were no street signs. A person could live Off-Broadway and avoid their creditors indefinitely. But Bo Hargis was a marked man with his shiny new SUV sitting next to one of the single-wides.

Junior and I watched the front, parked fifty feet or so down the street. The boys from Rockford covered the rear.

We had two choices. Either knock on the door and confront Bo, or like in a Jimmy Cagney movie, use a megaphone and call to him, "Okay, Hargis, this is the police. We've got you surrounded. Come out with your hands up, or we're comin' in to get ya!"

To that, he'd say, "Come and get me, you dirty coppers. You'll never take me alive!"

Although I have a flare for the dramatic, I walked up and knocked on the door.

"Who is it?" he asked through the closed door.

Then came the part I always hate. "Police officer, Mr. Hargis, I need to speak with you."

There was a moment of silence.

"Hang on a minute. I'll put on a pair of pants."

Junior and I looked at each other. I'm naturally impatient—and suspicious. Then the door opened. *Damn, he was big.* I held up my badge to identify myself. Junior stood there in uniform.

"What can I do for you boys?" Hargis spoke with only a hint of a Southern accent and looked like a professional wrestler. Along with the blue jeans he told us he needed to put on, he had added a navy blue sport jacket over his T-shirt. I guess he really wanted to spruce up for our visit.

"We have to speak with you about a Mrs. Ella Swope," I said. "Can we come in?"

He didn't answer immediately. After a few seconds of watching him, I assumed he was sizing us up. Big guys like Hargis often use their size to get out of jams. And ex-cons rarely believe a flimsy line like the one I used. I waited for him to make a move.

He brought his left hand up to rub his chin like he was thinking. But that was only to draw my attention. As he did so, I saw the stag grip and case-hardened frame of Danny Swope's single action Colt peek out from under his sport jacket.

I reached for my Smith and Wesson and yelled, "Gun!"

Junior hit the screen door with his shoulder so hard he broke the safety chain and one hinge. Hargis backed up into the dinette area. Instead of raising his hands, he moved for the gun.

The barrel just cleared his waistband as I squeezed off my first shot. It struck his chest. I double-tapped him with a second shot an inch to the left.

Junior fired twice; the sharp crack of my .38 contrasted with the throaty bark of the kid's .40 caliber Glock automatic. His second ejected cartridge struck my cheek. It felt warm on my skin. Hargis was down and out. No more wrestling or gun fighting for him.

Junior and I stood over the body. I stepped on the revolver in Bo's hand and pushed it away from him with my foot, my pistol still pointed at his head.

I lay two fingers across his carotid artery feeling for a pulse—nothing. I looked up at Junior and shook my head.

"Lord have mercy." The kid spoke quietly. "Why'd he do that?"

"Who knows? Maybe he didn't want to be labeled a three-time loser." I shrugged and stood up. "You okay?" I asked. That was Junior's first shooting.

He nodded and again softly said, "Lord have mercy."

Both Rockford cops burst in the door with their guns drawn.

Murn looked at Hargis, then at us. "Y'all okay?"

"Yeah, we're fine," I said.

Cody said, "Damn, he's a big'un."

I nodded.

"He dead?" the chief asked.

"Oh, yeah."

"I guess I'd better start makin' phone calls. You care if I use the Sheriff's people to write this up?"

"No, it's your town. We're okay. This one's nice and clean."

"I kin see." He pointed to the old west revolver lying on the linoleum floor.

The two Rockford cops walked outside to call the county dicks, the crime scene guys and the medical examiner.

Junior looked down at the body again. Four holes in a small group marked the center of Bo's broad chest. Blood covered the white T-shirt.

"Four Xs," I said. "You scored them when it really counted, kid."

"I guess." He didn't sound convinced.

"Look, that's your job. I know how you feel, but he cast his own fate. You did what you had to do. You owe it to me and your family to get home safely each day. Don't worry about what someone else says to you. This was a clean and justified shooting."

"I understand...I guess." He still didn't sound convinced.

"No, kid, I don't think you do." I wanted to drive home an important message. "I remember being at a big combat match in Jackson, Mississippi about thirty years ago. A tall lanky border patrolman—a pretty famous guy in the shooting circle—and I were talking. He said, 'Son, always remember, there ain't no second place winners in a gunfight.' Today we won, and Hargis came in second."

* * * *

After a quick stop in front of the grand jury, Junior and I sat in the hall of the Justice Center waiting to hear our fate. After only several minutes, the court officer came out smiling. He informed us that the shooting was officially designated 'justified'.

Junior took the rest of the day off. I went back to the PD.

When I walked in, I found Bettye sitting at my desk, thumbing through a loose-leaf binder full of monthly vehicle reports.

"You look good as the police chief," I said.

"Thank you, sir, but I'm happy where I am."

I smiled at her and thought she looked nice. Her blonde ponytail rested on her left shoulder; her hazel eyes sparkled.

"You look happy enough," she said. "Do I need to ask what happened?"

I shook my head. She smiled.

"You know," she said, changing the subject. "Bobby Crockett gets his car washed more than anyone else?"

"Bobby's a neat-freak. Does that mess up our budget?"

"It sure doesn't help."

"You want to scold him, or shall I?"

"Sometimes we sound like parents," she said.

"You're a good mother. Sometimes I wonder about my fatherly talents."

"You're doin' just fine, darlin'."

"Maybe I'll ask his Uncle Stanley to have a talk with him."

"Poor Stanley."

"Stanley is happy enough."

"Is our son, Junior, happy though?" she asked. "He doin' alright?"

"No, he's not. I can understand that, but he's got to get over this and move on."

"Have you spoken to him about seeing...our friend?" she asked.

Bettye referred to a psychotherapist who'd helped the department before.

"Peggy?"

"Uh-huh."

"Yeah, he's got an appointment."

"Good. And how about you? You okay, Sammy?"

I nodded. "Yeah, I'm fine. Hargis was a dirt bag. I'd feel worse if we shot a dog."

Bettye frowned and shook her head. "I wish you wouldn't say stupid things like that."

"They just come out so naturally."

I smiled again. She wrinkled up her nose and made a face at me.

"Do you think the citizens of Prospect could survive a day if we went to lunch at the same time?" she asked.

"Easy enough to arrange. I'm the boss."

"Well, boss-man, I'd like to buy you lunch."

"Sergeant, it would be my pleasure to have lunch with you, but I'll buy."

"Not this time, Sammy, and no arguments."

I have trouble arguing when she smiles at me.

"Okay, I'll buy a bottle of wine."

She frowned again. "Did you always drink while you were working?"

"Of course not! I waited until I was eighteen."

THE END

Scrap Metal and Murder

Wayne Zurl

Scrap Metal and Murder
Wayne Zurl

Gold is for the mistress—silver for the maid—
Copper for the craftsman, cunning at his trade.
"Good!" said the baron, sitting in his hall,
"But iron—cold iron—is master of them all."
Rudyard Kipling

Ned's Bucket O' Blood. The name suggested a real class joint. The Bucket, a typical Southern roadhouse, sat on a secondary highway, about fifty feet off the blacktop in a dog-eared neighborhood.

Large clumps of Dallisgrass dotted the gravel parking lot, and a bumper crop of ragweed grew along the exterior walls of the bar.

A half-dozen vehicles, four of them old pickup trucks, were scattered around the lot in no particular order. I parked near the door and walked in.

The smell of stale beer and old cigarette smoke could have gagged a maggot.

The occupants of those six parked vehicles perched on stools and lounged at tables throughout the dingy gin mill.

A not-quite-pretty blonde in a short black dress sang her rendition of *It Takes Balls to be a Woman*. Her guitarist wore a fancy two-tone cowboy shirt and looked vaguely like Stephen King, if Steve hadn't washed his hair in a decade.

I took a stool at the close end of the bar.

"What'll ya have?" the bartender asked as he dropped a stained coaster in front of me.

I placed him somewhere between forty and sixty, broad and short with a crew cut and a walrus mustache. From the twists of his nose, you could count the number of times it had been broken. His teeth were stained yellow as were two fingers of his right hand. He might have single-handedly accounted for the nicotine stink inside the Bucket O' Blood.

"What do you have on tap?" I asked.

"Bud."

"That's it?" I gave him a friendly smile.

"Uh-huh." He didn't return the smile.

"How about in a bottle?"

"Bud Light…an' more Bud."

"A company man, huh?" I managed another smile.

"Do what?" Still the same blank expression from him.

So far, a tip was out of the question.

"I'll have a pint of Bud."

"Don't got no pints."

"Okay, make it easy on yourself." I'd grown tired of our erudite debate.

He took three steps to the tap handle and came back with a twelve-ounce mug.

The beer was cold and fresh. The bartender went to check on his other customers, and I looked over the room. It probably wasn't the worst place I'd ever seen, but it made my bottom ten.

As the blonde ended her song, the barman walked back toward me, drying a glass.

"Are you Ned?" I asked.

"Nope, I'm Jake. Ned won't be here till mebbe eight-thirty, nine o'clock."

"Got a few minutes to talk?"

"Ain't exactly got a crowd takin' up my time," he said.

"I need some information."

My statement caused a wrinkle on his brow and a general look of distrust to alter his expression.

"You the po-leece or sumthin'?"

"Or something," I said and showed him my badge. "You know a guy named Melvin Kite? I understand he comes here."

94

"Melvin Kite? Hmm, not sure."

Jake's momma taught him how to play hard-to-get.

"How much was that beer?" I asked.

"Two-fifty."

I took a twenty from the folded wad of cash in my pocket and placed it on the bar.

I grinned and said, "I guess you could keep the change…if you knew something about this Melvin Kite guy."

Jake liked that idea. Finally, his turn to smile.

He scratched his chin. "Melvin Kite? Melvin Kite?" I guess he wanted me to think he was searching the inner recesses of his mind. "Sounds familiar now. He a short, stocky guy with a scar on his chin?"

"Sounds like my man, but the picture of him I saw was almost five years old."

"I know him," Jake said. "What's he done?"

"I'm not sure he's done anything," I lied. "Someone reported a hit-and-run and gave his plate number. I need to find him and straighten out that business."

"Why don't you go to his home?"

Jake was a practical thinker.

"All the addresses I can find are old. Melvin moves around a lot."

"Comes in here some," Jake said, "exspecially when they's live music. I 'spect he'll be here tonight ta see Marla."

He used his chin as a pointer and gestured toward the stage where the blonde flipped through the pages of a spiral notebook, and Stephen King tuned his guitar.

"You've been a big help, Jake," I said.

He took hold of the twenty with his thumb and forefinger. I grabbed the opposite end and tugged. I won.

"I done thought you said…" Jake looked surprised and disappointed.

I tore the twenty in half, gave one part to Jake and filed the second half in my top pocket.

"Give me a wink, Jake, old buddy, when Mr. Kite shows up. Then the other half's yours. Okay?"

Jake nodded. He liked that idea, too.

I looked at my watch: 7:30. I had some waiting to do. I picked up

Jake's copy of the News-Sentinel and took that and my beer to a table in the far corner of the room. There wasn't much light to read by, so I looked at the pictures.

Marla and Steve started playing again, something with a Nashville sound. I heard lyrics about a cheatin' man, a pickup and possibly a ratchet wrench, but I'm terrible at music comprehension.

At 8 p.m., a stocky, blue-collar guy dressed in the ubiquitous outfit of the Smokies walked into Ned's. Washed-off blue jeans rode low on his wide hips. A faded orange UT jersey hung outside his pants, and a dirty Atlanta Braves ball cap sat on his head.

He bellied up to the bar and grabbed the mug of Bud Jake had ready for him. After taking a sip, he did a right face and stepped over to an unoccupied table.

I looked at Jake. He put a finger up to his nose and nodded. My twenty-dollar signal. He must have learned that gesture from Paul Newman in *The Sting*.

I folded the paper, picked up my mug and headed toward the bar. I dropped my half of the twenty on the counter, winked at Jake and touched my nose. Robert Redford all the way.

After waiting thirty seconds for Marla to finish her song, I took a short walk to Melvin's table and sat down.

He swiveled his head and gave me a surprised look.

"Hi," I said, "I'll bet you're Melvin Kite."

"Do what?" was the best he came up with.

"My name's Jenkins, but you can call me Chief—as in police chief—from beautiful downtown Prospect, Tennessee."

"I ain't done nuthin'," he said, shifting in his chair to look at me square on.

The dark hair sticking out from under his cap needed a trim, and his five o'clock shadow looked several hours old.

"Sure you have, Melvin," I said. "Let's start out on the right foot. I won't bullshit you, so don't bullshit me. Okay?"

"What the hell ya talkin' about?"

"Copper, Melvin. I'm talking about copper."

"Oh," he said, and his shoulders dropped three inches.

"Where'd you get all the copper you've been selling at Knoxville

Scrap Metal and Salvage?"

"I ain't sold much there, not but a few pounds."

"Goddamnit, Melvin. Now you've gone and pissed me off. I thought we had a no-bullshit treaty."

He frowned at that.

"If we weren't in a public place," I said, "I'd have taken offense to that lie and smacked you upside the head with this mug of beer. Wanna try answering that question again?"

He let his chin drop and looked at the mug he held between his two hands. "Whatcha wanna know?"

"The salvage yard has records of you bringing in hundreds of pounds of copper. Where'd you get it?"

"I guess ya done already figgered that out."

"Yeah, ya think?"

Marla started another tune, and Steve closed his eyes as he strummed his guitar.

"Now, Melvin, why don't we listen to the young lady sing about her shithead boyfriend, finish our beers, then take a ride to my office and talk about your midnight scrap metal business?"

* * * *

The parking spots next to the PD back door allow us to walk suspects and prisoners inside without giving them much chance to escape. I used one when Melvin Kite and I pulled in behind the Municipal building.

We bypassed the squad room, and I led Melvin directly to my office. We sat in the guest chairs in front of my desk and faced each other. I didn't offer to make coffee.

"Okay, Melvin," I said, "let's talk copper."

"Shoot, ya already know how much I sold. I'm guessin' Scotty done tol' ya he figgered it was me doin' the stealin'."

"Yeah, I knew you were taking the copper. You tell me why."

"Why?" The question came out incredulously. "Fer cash, that's why. The war's done drove the price o' copper sky high. It was quick cash, is all."

"And you chose to screw Scotty Beets, the guy who paid you a regular salary?"

"Weren't nuthin' personal. I figgered either the people we's buildin' the houses fer or Scotty, one, got them in-surance."

My ability to quote answers like that would sound good in court if he refused to plea bargain.

"Have you got an attorney?"

"Me?"

I took that as a negative answer.

"I guess you'll ask for a public defender?"

"I guess."

"I'll make life easy for you, Melvin. If you write out a statement and admit to stealing the copper, I'll talk to the DA for you and recommend they work with your lawyer, give you the best deal possible."

"I don't think I wanna put nuthin' in writin'." He shook his head. His expression made me think he'd been down that road before.

"You only get one chance for a good deal. You say no tonight, and I say no when your free lawyer asks to knock this down to misdemeanor larceny and let you do your time close to home."

"I ain't writin' no confession. Do what ya gotta do."

Smug bastard. I felt like smacking him.

"Okay, stand up. You're under arrest. Turn around. Handcuff time."

I thought he was an asshole, but I didn't say it.

* * * *

Two hours and a short drive later, I walked Melvin through the back door of the county sheriff's pre-arraignment detention facility at the Justice Center in neighboring Maryville. A corrections sergeant named Charlie Whittaker took my paperwork while another CO unhooked my cuffs from Melvin's wrists and handed them back to me.

"Hey there, Mr. Sam," Charlie said, "got ya another local villain ta see the judge?"

"Not exactly John Dillinger, Sarge, but he's all I could come up with on short notice," I said, just to be personable.

"I hear that," he said.

He handed me a receipt for my prisoner, smiled and nodded, prompting his accomplice to take my villain away.

"Behave yourself, Melvin," I said. "Charlie, good doing business with you. I hope you're keeping track of how many customers I bring you. After every dozen, I win a toaster oven, right?"

He laughed. "Shoot, not hardly."

"This cop's life's not worth living anymore, is it?" I turned and waved good-bye.

As my left foot hit the blacktop parking lot, the heavens opened up. Who takes a prisoner into the county jail with an umbrella tucked under his arm?

"Son of a bitch!" I said to no one in particular.

As I ran toward my car, I felt the stuffy humidity of a late summer storm envelope me. The air smelled like a wet cat. The windbreaker I wore to hide my holstered Smith and Wesson quickly became soaked. I was not a happy policeman.

I pulled to a stop at the traffic light across from Blount Memorial Hospital. With no other cars in sight, I turned right onto US 321 and headed for home, thinking uncompensated overtime sucked.

* * * *

Scotty Beets walked into my office at quarter-after-nine the next morning.

He looked as skinny as a snake and showed limitless nervous energy, constantly turning and twisting in his chair.

Beets had the reputation of being one of the better and more honest building contractors in the county.

His blond hair looked like he had it cut by Buster Brown's barber.

It might take you a week of careful listening, but soon enough most people learn the different accents of East Tennessee—flatlanders versus mountain folk. Scotty spoke with the nasal twang of a flatlander.

He reached forward and dropped a manila folder on my blotter.

"Here's the lists o' all the copper taken from my job sites," he said. "Got the dates and amounts, best as I kin tell."

"Thanks. The scrap metal dealer wants to cooperate. It should be easy to match up what's missing to what Melvin sold."

"Good. Ya think I'll git any o' that material back?"

"Hard to say. Maybe…if it's not already crushed up."

99

"Damn that Melvin Kite."

"He wouldn't sign a confession, so he'll most likely make bail sometime today. If he shows up at one of your sites to talk or he gives you any trouble, call 9-1-1."

"He won't give me no trouble, nosir. And I bet he jest might wanna steal him some more copper 'fore he goes ta jail. I'll lay low and keep an eye on the job with the most copper. I'll catch him in the act. *Then* I'll call 9-1-1."

I just love the vigilante mentality.

"Scotty, this is only copper we're talking about. No sense getting into a confrontation over it. Let us do all the police work."

"I treated that man good. He had no reason ta steal from me. Man's not a good Christian."

"That might be so, but why go to that trouble yourself? You'll have your opportunity to testify against him. Beat him in court. You're a key person in the case. You'll get your pound of flesh."

"The man will not steal from me ag'in."

Scotty Beets walked out of my office mad at Melvin Kite and perhaps the world in general.

* * * *

Two days later, Kate and I were out of bed at seven o'clock, and by eight, we had breakfast on the table. In the middle of my bowl of All-Bran, the phone rang. I looked at the caller ID and answered.

"Vernon," I said, looking at my watch, "it's not even quarter-after-eight. Why are you calling me?"

"Hey, boss, you doin' aw rot today?"

PO Vern Hobbs didn't wait for an answer to that question. No one ever does.

"Sorry ta bother ya," he said," but we got us a homo-cide."

He made it sound like someone's sexual preference.

"Why me, Vernon? Why do people get killed in my jurisdiction? I'm getting too old for this."

"Damned if I know, Sam. But this one probably won't be too hard ta figger out. A workman called it in. Scotty Beets got hisse'f kilt last night."

100

* * * *

By the time I reached the construction site on Breckenridge Drive, the county crime scene investigators had the partially completed home cordoned off with yellow police line tape.

I hopped up on the cheek of an unfinished stoop and entered the future living room.

CSI David Sparks walked bent over, scrutinizing the plywood subfloor. An array of evidence bags stuck out of his back pocket. He held a pair of large tweezers in his hand.

"What do you say, Sparky?" I said.

"Hey, Chief, you doin' aw rot today?"

He really wasn't waiting for an answer either, so I walked over to where Vern Hobbs stood looking down into the cutout for the future cellar stairs.

"Hey, boss," he said, "body's down here."

He pointed into the basement. An aluminum extension ladder protruded from the hole. At the bottom, I saw a yellow throwaway police blanket covering all but a pair of white socks and ten-inch work boots.

"How did he die?"

"He got him a good ol' crack on the side o' his head. Look yonder. They's a length o' iron rebar with blood on it. Cain't say if the whack kilt him or the fall. Got a big scrape on the forehead, too. Musta fell square on his head."

"What else you know?"

"Not much. He musta been hidin' here last night, ta catch him that copper thief in the act. His white Ty-ota Highlander's parked in the trees, hunnert yards up the road a'piece."

I opened my cell phone, called the Sheriff's office and asked for the admin clerk at the jail. From her I learned that Melvin Kite arranged for bail after his arraignment and had been out and about since then.

"Where's the ME?" I asked.

"Gonna be a while. Some old man died in his sleep over ta Rockford. Family doctor won't sign no death certificate, so Doc Rappaport's over there."

"That Jackie Shuman I hear downstairs?"

"Yep, he's doin what Sparky's doin' up here."

I descended the ladder gingerly, hoping the damn thing didn't slide on the newly burnished cement and send me falling like a moron on top of the corpse.

Fate was good. I reached the basement with the proper amount of class. Jackie Shuman, the other CSI, looked over.

"Hey, Sam, you doin' aw rot today?"

"You interrupted my breakfast, young man. What have you got to help me solve this mess?"

"Beats me. You know how much odds an' ends an' do-dads are layin' around a construction site? Already got me a bunch o' li'l bags full o' things that probably won't mean nuthin'."

"Our life's not easy, Jack. When you're finished, bring all that over to the office, and I'll look at it."

"You got it, bud."

Back on ground level, I asked Vern, "Who else is working today?"

"Lenny's got the town sector and Junior's doin' the west end."

"Tell Lenny to stay on the road and handle all the calls unless things get busy. You and Junior do a neighborhood canvas and see if anyone knows anything. Go pretty far afield in case a jogger or dog walker passed by."

Vern scratched his grizzled gray hair and shook his head.

"I got me the worst luck o' any cop in the world. In thirty-three years, I ain't never found one good witness ta nuthin'."

Vern only stood about five-foot-five, but had the look of a tough old bandy rooster.

"Think how I felt working in New York," I said. "I did some neighborhood investigations where I was the only guy who spoke English."

"That's the reason I ain't never wanted ta leave east Tennessee. Wait now, I tell a lie. I done took the wife over ta Myrtle Beach once't."

I didn't laugh, but told Vern, "Hold down the fort. I've got to see a fat man about some copper."

* * * *

Melvin Kite lived in a single-wide along Old-Piney Road in

102

Maryville.

He didn't exactly have a lot of hot employment prospects, so finding him at home seemed like a good bet.

Melvin's live-in girlfriend, a blonde named Delphine Studsill, was with him. She said she worked the three-to-eleven shift at the Wal-Mart Supercenter in Alcoa.

Kite showed no hostility when I asked to speak with him. We sat in the TV room, and I scanned the surroundings. The place looked like five rooms in search of a personality. It made a Motel 6 look homey.

Delphine seemed a little younger than Melvin's forty-nine years. Actually attractive, she wore her age with more grace than Melvin did. While not exactly pretty, she had a good face and showed much more intelligence than her roommate. She may have been overdue for her appointment with Lady Clairol, but alongside the dumpy Melvin, she fit like a half-dollar in a nickel slot.

I decided to take the direct approach and break the news to Melvin.

"Scotty Beets has been murdered."

His mouth fell open. Delphine stopped puttering around in the adjoining kitchen. She set down the coffee pot she'd been drying and looked at me.

"You were quick to lawyer up the other day. Want him here now, or will you answer a few questions?"

He frowned and thought for a long moment.

"Don't need no lawyer fer this one."

Kite took a pack of Marlboros from his shirt pocket and lit up. Delphine came over and sat on the sofa next to her beau. She took a skinny brown cigarette from a pack of Virginia Slims lying on the coffee table and ignited it with a Bic lighter.

In less than five minutes, the smoke gave me a headache. I should have taken a different job.

"Okay, tell me where you've been since you made bail," I said.

Melvin wrapped up a neat package for me. He offered nothing that would make me feel secure if a potential murder charge hung over my head, but he could account for his time. Most of it included Delphine—if I could believe her.

* * * *

Looking for the quickest way back to the Municipal building, I jumped onto US 321 heading east. From the highway, a solid wall of fog stood defiantly to the west. Directly overhead, I saw clear sky and a bright morning sun. Then to the east, lacy white clouds hung just a hundred feet above the roadway in the Walland Gap. Those are some of the visual benefits you enjoy by living in the mountains.

I took a shortcut through the old community of Cold Springs. On a winding country road, I passed the Mountain View Congregational Church. On the bulletin board out front, someone had posted a biblical sentiment. "Quench not the spirit. 1 Thessalonians 5:19". To me it sounded like the motto of some Army unit. Might work for a Civil Affairs brigade.

I pulled into our PD parking area and found a Sheriff's office crime scene van sitting in one of the spots. Inside, Jackie and David presented me with a cardboard box full of small evidence bags, all gathered from the basement and first floor of the murder scene. I thanked them and, lacking the energy to go through it, locked everything in our evidence closet.

* * * *

After a late lunch at Howell's Pub, I began the drive back to the office. Sitting at the traffic light on McTeer's Station Pike and South Main, my cell phone went off. The Rolling Stones treated me to a quick version of *Paint it Black.* I pulled into the parking lot of Johnny Milton's Paradise Found Steak House and answered.

Hearing Moira Menzies, the chief assistant district attorney for Blount County, on the other end surprised me. She never calls my cell phone.

"Sam," she said, "I just heard Scott Beets was killed the other night. I have information for you that may be important to your investigation."

She explained that Beets testified twice before a special grand jury. Calvin Pitts, the current DA, had a year to go before reelection and decided to have his people make a full court press on things illegal in the county and give voters something to remember at the polls.

"You know who R. Wade Butterbaugh is?" she asked.

"Sure, the local king of affordable housing."

"More or less, yes. Scott Beets had been his overall foreman up until a couple of years ago when he went out on his own." She paused.

That interesting fact didn't mean much at the moment, but I wanted to hear where she intended to go with the conversation.

"Uh-huh?"

"Oh, Lord, don't you read the papers?" she said with a little exasperation.

"Not unless Robert B. Parker has something new out."

"Lord have mercy, Sam. You're impossible."

"Thanks. I love you, too."

"Please listen, and learn something. We've been investigating Butterbaugh as one of the biggest employers of undocumented aliens and for at least a half dozen violations of the General Business Law. Scotty Beets agreed to blow the whistle on Butterbaugh."

She said all that like I knew nothing of the world around me. Moira likes to verbally stick it to me whenever she can.

"Is Butterball looking at serious penalties if you convict him?"

"For God sakes, Sam, it's Butterbaugh and yes, more than serious. Between local and federal penalties, he would end up broke. Jail time isn't out of the question either."

"Have you got a slam dunk here?"

"Pretty close. Immigration investigators raided a couple of his construction sites and bagged a truckload of undocumented Mexicans. ICE seized his books. We've monitored any state violations to his contractor's responsibilities and weeded out the civil suit possibilities and still have him for numerous indictable misdemeanors. With Beets' firsthand knowledge of his intent, he'd have been toast."

"And Scotty was enthusiastic about testifying?"

"Yes, and we had no interest in listening to a plea bargain. Now, without Beets, I'm not so sure."

"Okay, point taken," I said. "R. Wade must be quite happy that old Scotty is out of commission."

"My thoughts exactly. I wanted you to know."

"And I thank you profusely, madam. You're my all-time favorite

DA. Love and kisses."

"Sam, I doubt anyone loves you. Call me if you learn anything interesting."

* * * *

For two days, the Widow Beets surrounded herself with grieving relatives who claimed she was under a doctor's care and unable to be questioned. I saw that as unusual.

On the day before Scotty's funeral, my time became valuable, and Linda Beets had to face the music.

Unfortunately, this conductor proved unable to get Mrs. Beets to sing much.

I learned she spent her first twenty-five years in Michigan. For three years after finishing college, she worked for The Ford Motor Company. From there, she landed a job with the Nippon Denso Corporation, a manufacturer of auto parts based in Maryville, Tennessee—one of Blount County's major employers. After five years with Denso, as it's now called, she married Scott. Twelve years and two children later, we sat in her living room, discussing her dead husband.

But the discussion lead nowhere. Other than recognizing her as an attractive brunette and not an airhead, she seemed as helpful as swim fins in a blizzard.

* * * *

My next stop: R. Wade Butterbaugh's office. Only R. Wade wasn't there, and according to his wife, Cassie Butterbaugh, he wouldn't talk to me anyway without his lawyer.

This will not go down as one of my easier investigations.

"I know this is going to be futile, Mrs. Butterbaugh," I said, "but could you call the lawyer, and let me speak to him?"

"Please," she said with a dazzling smile, "call me Cassie. I know you're only doing your job. There's no reason for us to be overly formal…or enemies."

"Okay, Cassie, as you can see on that nifty business card the City of Prospect printed up for me, I'm Sam. I hate formalities, too, and I certainly don't want to be anyone's enemy."

That was a ridiculous load of manure, but I felt obligated to smile and say so.

"Well, good, Sam. Sit down here with me." She patted an armchair next to her desk. "And I'll call Wade's lawyer. His name's Brack Clemons."

I said Linda Beets was attractive. Cassie Butterbaugh qualified as a real fox, Hollywood material. I had a great morning finding good-looking women; I just needed some luck nailing a killer.

I sat, and Cassie shot me a million-dollar smile. She took off an old-fashioned, gold clip-on earring and nestled the telephone next to her chewable ear. She punched in seven digits, a local number.

I vaguely heard the ring on the other end. I looked at Cassie. She looked at me. We both smiled.

I'd run her on the Motor Vehicle computer for a date of birth, but I figured her for mid-forties. I also figured her for three days a week at a local gym, once a week at a beauty shop to do up her auburn hair, and I'd bet a New York pension check she bought her clothes at Dillard's and not Kmart.

She spoke into the phone and waited, smiled at me again, and waited some more.

Finally, "Here ya go, sugar," she said and handed me the phone.

R. Wade's mouthpiece made it short and sweet. His client had nothing to say.

I refused to call that strike three. I had one more errand to run before I left Maryville and returned to Prospect.

* * * *

Five minutes later, I sat in front of Claude Lawson, my insurance broker.

"Are you sure these people will give me at least sixty grand if my Healey is stolen or totaled? I asked.

"Far as I can tell," he said, "a 1967 BJ8, as you call it, in mint condition, is the most desirable and collectible Austin-Healey on the market. Watch the auctions, and document a couple of sales each year. If, God forbid, something happens, you've got a sales history to fall back on."

Claude is only two years older than I am, but his snow-white hair tacked on another five years to his looks.

"Okay, Claude, I'm putting my faith in you."

He grinned and accepted my check. The Healey, my F-150 and Kate's Subaru would be covered for another six months.

"Shame 'bout Scotty Beets, ain't it?" he said.

"Yeah. How do you know him?"

"From church. He was a deacon."

"You two friends?"

"Friendly enough. He has his insurance with us."

"Were the materials at his job sites insured against loss? You know—fire, theft? All that?"

"Lord have mercy, no. A policy like that would cost an arm and a leg. It's expensive ta insure unsecured building materials. He has homeowner's and auto policies from us."

"Know of anyone who disliked Scotty?"

"No, he was a nice enough feller, but I guess all things considered, he *was* messin' with fire."

That remark piqued my interest.

"You mean testifying against Wade Butterbaugh?" I asked.

"No, Sam. I mean havin' that affair with Cassie Butterbaugh."

* * * *

Another fifteen minutes later and I knocked on the raised panel door that separated the Butterbaugh suite from the hall of the professional building housing their offices. No answer. I tried again.

My racket brought an old gent around the corner. He wore a dark blue custodian's uniform. His name tag read Otis.

"Makin' a li'l noise here, ain't ya?" he said.

I palmed my shield and showed him.

"Sorry to disturb you and the other tenants, but I've had one shitty day and finding out Mrs. Butterbaugh just disappeared is icing on the cake."

"I seen you leave before. Figgered you's the po-leece. Couple minutes after you left, the receptionist—her name's Tammy—she leaves. Mrs. B's rot behind her."

108

* * * *

Several big shade trees rimmed the parking lot behind Butterbaugh's office building. I sat there in my car, trying to make some headway on the phone.

Ma Bell must have been on sabbatical that afternoon. No one answered my calls. Except my wife—she promised to have a very large drink ready when I got home.

I pulled into the Municipal lot and saw Vern Hobbs gassing his car. I parked and walked over.

"Hey, boss, you doin' aw rot today?"

"Don't ask, Vernon."

"Uh-oh."

"Find anything when you and Junior did the neighborhood canvas?"

"Not a helluva lot. The kid's got a list o' ve-hickles we seen and anythin' somebody else said they seen."

"When you go back into service, tell Junior to drop it off before he goes home."

* * * *

The back door to the PD slammed as I entered. I made a mental note to have someone adjust the pneumatic closer. After trudging down the hall, I entered my office, took off my jacket, tossed it at the closest guest chair—and missed. It's a good thing the custodial staff keeps my floor clean.

I pulled the cardboard box of potential evidentiary items out of the locked closet. Shuman and Sparks provided me with more little plastic and paper evidence bags and envelopes than I wanted to count.

I carried the box down to the squad room, set up our extra eight-foot folding table and began to spread out everything I needed to look at in my search for clues.

Most of what I saw looked like nothing but a bunch of crap. Construction workers are not known for their tidiness.

I pushed all the sixteen-penny nails over with the ten-penny nails, which already lay there with the nail gun nails.

The Sheriff's vacuum cleaner provided several bags of saw dust, wood shavings, wire insulation scraps, tufts of fiberglass insulation—you get the idea.

I segregated the dozens of cigarette filters, other tidbits I couldn't place but knew had some construction value, and a few filthy, stepped-on business cards.

One item I couldn't identify stood out like prunes on a pizza. In a small, clear plastic bag, a tiny white rubber cylinder waited for me to find a purpose for it, but I'd be damned if I could. Branded with David Sparks' initials, the bag also showed his badge number, the date and our case number.

A tiny hole marked the center of the cylinder. The hole looked much too small to accommodate any electrical wire, and the rubber was different from the insulation on the typically thin telephone wire.

Baffled and hungry and still at work after five o'clock, I decided to pack up all the extraneous clues and again lock them in the evidence closet.

I did something no world-class detective should never do; I stuck the bag with the little rubber thingie in my pocket and went home.

* * * *

Standing in our kitchen, Kate said, "Here you go, my dear. Sounds like you had a Glenfiddich kind of day." She handed me a short glass with two cubes and three fingers of amber-colored liquid.

"You better believe it, sweetie." I accepted the drink gratefully. "I see you've made my cocktail a large one."

"Yes, sir. About three ounces of the finest Aberdeenshire whisky."

"You're not only beautiful, but useful. What's for dinner?"

"Smoked salmon in a light Alfredo sauce over pasta with a tomato and artichoke salad."

"And who says Polish girls can't cook?"

"Hey, watch it. Do I make snide remarks about how much you Scottish people drink?"

"Okay, Miss Smarty-pants. It's show and tell time," I said. "I show you something. You tell me what it is."

"What do I get if I guess correctly?"

"My undying gratitude."

"Not enough. That's what you tell all the girls."

"Don't push your luck."

I placed the evidence bag on the kitchen counter. Kate turned the bag over and looked at the object for a few seconds.

"I thought you had a tough question, Sherlock."

"Don't toy with me, Watson. Out with it."

"Haven't you ever seen an earring keeper before?"

"I know lighthouse keepers, zoo keepers and gate keepers, but not earring keepers."

"For a genius, you are so obtuse at times. Earring keepers keep earrings with French wires from falling off."

"Of course, why didn't I know that?"

"You're a man. You know nothing about women."

"Ha!"

* * * *

Frank and Joanne Muellenberg hired Scotty Beets to build the house where Scotty died.

Recently retired from Michigan, the Muellenbergs lived in a two-bedroom apartment on Topside Road in Louisville, a twenty-minute drive from Prospect.

"No, sir," Joanne, a chubby and happy-looking blonde, said. "I don't use earring keepers. Fact is, I don't use other than posts, and they have their own little clutch-back doohickeys to keep them on my ears."

I showed her the rubber earring keeper.

"So this couldn't be yours?"

"No, I've never owned anything like that."

Then who was the female who lost her earring keeper?

"Do you folks have builder's insurance on the structure and materials at the job site?"

"No," Frank said, sounding a little surprised. "I never thought about that. This is the first place we've built. You think we'll have to eat the cost of the stuff that got stolen a few weeks back?"

"I don't know what your contract says. Might be a moot point now that the builder is dead."

They looked at each other and frowned.

"One last question," I said. "Do either of you smoke?"

111

They both shook their heads.

* * * *

Not only an insurance salesman, my buddy, Claude Lawson was also a card-carrying cop buff. I stepped into his office and dumped a half dozen police shoulder patches on his desk—a bribe.

"Well, look at that," he said with a big smile. "Where'd you git those?"

"Here and there. Some cops collect them. Guys who do usually give you one of theirs and ask for one of yours in return. I've accumulated them over the years. I thought you'd like them."

"Thank ya, Sam. I appreciate that. You know I just love what you boys do ta keep us all safe and pro-tected."

"Better not forget the girls who keep you safe—they get equal time nowadays."

He smiled again.

"Let's do some investigating together, Claude," I said. "Tell me more about Scotty Beets' affair with Cassie Butterbaugh."

* * * *

I opened the front door of the Butterbaugh Building and saw Otis buffing the shiny tile floor. With only a tilt of his wrist, the machine changed directions, and the big round pad slid from one side of the hall to the other. He saw me and stopped the buffer.

"Mornin'," he said.

I nodded. "How's it goin'?"

"Fair."

"She wouldn't happen to be upstairs, would she?" I figured he'd know I was looking for the lovely Cassie.

"Shore is," he said grinning. "Probably jest waitin' fer ya."

I pointed my finger at him and let my thumb fall like the hammer of a gun—a gesture Philip Marlowe called the gunman's salute.

The Butterbaugh's office occupied a large portion of the second floor. I opened the door. Cassie stood there next to Tammy, the secretary and receptionist.

"Why, good mornin', Sam," Cassie said with a big smile. "You doin' all right today?"

Tammy nodded and half smiled.

"Hello, ladies," I said. "Cassie, we need to talk."

Five minutes later, sitting in her private office, she said, "Oh, Lord have mercy. I am so embarrassed."

She looked lovely, charming, but not embarrassed.

"Cassie, did Wade catch you and Scotty together?"

"Good Lord, no," she said with a look of relief. "And, sugar, if he did, ol' Wade wouldn't hardly care."

My investigation wasn't getting any easier.

"Okay, clue me in. Why would he *not* care?"

"'Cause he's got his own girlfriends." She looked at me like I was a child having difficulty grasping a simple concept. "Wade and me haven't given a hoot 'bout each other for years. We stay married for the business—for the money, darlin'."

That *was* a difficult concept for me to grasp, but I tried not to skip a beat.

"The other day you wore clip-on earrings," I said. "What do you have on today?"

"Same thing, sugar. Why do you ask?"

"Take them off. Let me see."

"Do what?" Her big green eyes blinked at me.

"I want to see your earlobes."

"Oh. I thought…well, doesn't matter."

She unclipped the old-fashioned earrings. Her ears were not pierced.

* * * *

As I left Cassie and walked out into the sunshine, I had to say *strike four*. So far, the people involved in that fiasco led me nowhere. I drove back to the PD and looked at the list of vehicles Junior and Vern compiled.

The cars with plate numbers noted all came back to local residents who belonged in the neighborhood.

A few people offered descriptions of other cars they saw parked or traveling through the subdivision, but no one noticed those plate numbers.

So, I had three unidentified sedans and an SUV to match to someone.

Of course, one of the local residents could have offed Scotty Beets for some unknown reason, but that would have to stay on the back burner while I worked on those who had either proximity or motive.

Breckenridge Drive and several other privately maintained roads made up the gated community called Blackberry Valley. All the residents had a way to open the gates. Visitors and other interlopers were admitted differently. I called the Homeowner's Association president and twenty minutes later, found him waiting for me at the gates to the subdivision. I followed him back to his home.

Edd Bailey had been easy to contact. A retired banker, living alone, he stayed home much of the time, tending a garden and taking care of association business.

"We all have gate openers," he explained. "If, for some reason, the opener doesn't work, dead batteries or some other malfunction, we can punch in a six digit code and open the gates."

"How does a guest or worker get in?" I asked.

We sat on his deck, a long affair attached to the rear of his house and accessed from the dining room.

"Couple of ways. If they're regulars, people like exterminators, delivery drivers, whomever, they get their own code. If someone stops by to visit, they can use the keypad to find the resident's name and then click on it. That rings the phone at the resident's house. Punching a nine on the home phone automatically opens the gate."

"And how about temporary workers? Construction workers?" I said.

"The property owners tell us when they have a situation like that. They're building a house, putting on an addition, building a pool, whatever. I give them a temporary number. Short-term projects get numbers automatically cancelled out every thirty days. Home builders or long term people get up to six months before we change them."

"How about Scott Beets? He was building the Muellenberg's home."

"Sure, I know him. He had two numbers. One long-term number for him. As the general contractor, he would be around a long time. I gave him a second code for the subcontractors who would come and go."

As he spoke, I noticed two squirrels. One chased the other up and around an old tulip poplar. It must have been mating season.

"Sounds like a pretty good system," I said. "Can you keep track of who comes and goes?"

"We can. You've probably seen the sign about video surveillance cameras. Well, that's just a bluff. We have a fake camera mounted at the gate. But we do get a computer record of what codes are entered and when."

I felt a ray of hope tingle through me.

The frantic squirrels disappeared, but a pileated woodpecker blasted away on the trunk of a Virginia pine, sounding like short bursts from a .30 caliber light machinegun. Nature is not all that peaceful.

"I've got a list of four unaccounted-for vehicles in here the night Beets was murdered," I said. "Can you get me the info on who came through the gates that day?"

By using his computer, he could, and he did. Besides Scott Beets himself, homeowners buzzed in three vehicles. One other used the most current subcontractor's code, the code given to Scott Beets.

Telephone calls to the residents with guests accounted for three sedans roughly matching the descriptions Vern and Junior received. The SUV, which could have been a black, blue or dark green Ford, Mercury, or Chevy, had yet to be accounted for.

* * * *

I started banging away on the PD computer, running names through the Department of Safety motor vehicle files. R. Wade Butterbaugh drove a new Lexus LS-460. Cassie owned a red Mercedes SL500—my kind of girl. Melvin Kite's Dodge pickup didn't come close to anything seen that night. Linda and Scott Beets accounted for his white Toyota SUV and her Green Nissan Xterra. The Nissan came close, but not exactly the SUV described.

I wondered if Linda knew about Scott's affair with the lovely Cassie.

Then I remembered Melvin's girlfriend, Delphine Studsill. I ran her name and found a six-year-old, dark blue Mercury Mountaineer. Very close. Maybe fat Melvin borrowed her car.

All that proved very interesting. A sense of elation surged through my veins following that modicum of success. But no one was talking to me. I needed more than my suspicions and a vehicle close to a sketchy description. I needed to know more about Scotty Beets.

* * * *

"Claude," I said, back again in his insurance office, "I'm getting nowhere fast. Help me out here, partner. I need to know lots about the late Mr. Beets."

"Shoot, Sam, I've known him for years, but I don't really know him, if you know what I mean."

"I do. But let's look at this like cops. No answer is ever good enough."

"Do what?"

"You know him from going to the same church?"

"Uh-huh."

If you visited Claude during the cool months, he'd be wearing a jacket and tie. For the summer, he made do with a sport shirt and dress pants.

"So you see him every Sunday?" I asked.

"And Wednesday nights."

"Wednesdays, too?"

"Bible school and fellowship."

"Oh."

"But we weren't close friends...didn't socialize outside church."

"He must have had some friends. His wife is no damn help, and for that reason, I've got to look at her as a suspect."

"Lord have mercy." Claude sounded shocked that a wife might kill her husband.

"Right. I need to know Scott better. Who were his friends? What did he like to do? Did he play golf, go fishing...? Whatever."

Claude shifted in his big leather chair.

"He was a hiker. Mountain climber, too. Serious about it. Heard him talk about his trips couple o' times."

"Good, now we're getting somewhere. Can't be many mountain climbers around. What kind of mountains? Mount Everest and other exotic stuff?'"

Claude grinned. "I think more like the Smokies. Maybe down in North Georgia, North Carolina…more local."

"Did he have a climbing or hiking buddy, or did he belong to a club?"

"I think you should talk with Billy Joe Carpenter. He'd probably know something."

* * * *

After a fifteen-minute drive from Claude's office, I found the forty-something-year-old Billy Joe Carpenter in the community of Rocky Branch, in the shadow of Nebo Mountain.

When I pulled up to his home, I found him standing in his driveway working on a motorcycle that looked old enough to be something my father might have owned.

"Pretty old bike," I said.

"'48 Indian," he said. "Not many of these babies left."

He had a George Clooney, salt and pepper haircut. Billy Joe was a good-looking guy.

"Worth a lot of money?" I asked.

"Will be when I get finished restoring it."

"I need your help, Mr. Carpenter."

"About Scotty?"

"Yeah, I heard you two were friends."

"Shoot, me an' Scotty hiked a lot in the park and did a bunch o' miles on the A.T."

For those unfamiliar with the locale or hiker's lingo, the park is The Great Smoky Mountains National Park, and the A.T. is the Appalachian Trail.

"I guess you had plenty of time to talk?" I said.

"We did."

"Look, Mr. Carpenter, I know Scotty was having an affair, maybe more than one. Something like that could have a direct bearing on who killed him. I'd like you to tell me all you know."

"That makes me feel like I'd betray what I heard in confidence."

"I've got two things to say about that, sir. I believe Scotty would like his killer caught, and I'd think a churchgoing man like you would want to tell the truth."

He dropped the crescent wrench he held into a metal toolbox and wiped his hands with a clean rag. He raised his eyes to meet mine and nodded.

"WWJD?" he said.

"I beg your pardon?" I said.

"What would Jesus do?"

"Not much doubt about that, is there?"

"He'd do the right thing."

"Be my guess."

* * * *

I learned something. A guy like Billy Joe Carpenter turned to his religious hero, looking for guidance. And finally, he did the right thing.

I doubted He had much experience with criminal investigations, so I turned to another for *my* inspiration. What would Nero Wolfe do? One picture came to mind. Assemble the suspects, talk about what I knew, what I suspected, ask questions, and then see what happens? In the books and movies, the killer breaks down and confesses. It all sounded good in theory. I thought I'd give it a try.

* * * *

My first order of business was a phone call to my new friend, Cassie Butterbaugh. She still occupied a spot on my list of suspects, but that spot sat low on the totem pole. And she had a few tidbits of information that would make my life easier. One very interesting fact came from a conversation she once had with Scotty.

After ten minutes with Cassie, I called the rest of my players.

I scheduled the dog and pony show for ten the next morning. The cast included: The Butterbaughs: Cassie, R. Wade, their secretary, Tammy to take notes, and the attorney, Brack Clemons, to protect their rights.

Linda Beets, Scotty's not-so-grieving widow, told me she'd attend and bring her attorney, my old friend, Joe Costello.

Of course, I summoned Melvin Kite, who would bring Delphine

Studsill for moral support.

Billy Joe Carpenter agreed to show in case I needed to tap into his wealth of information on Scotty Beets.

Lastly, I figured Nero Wolfe would never assemble a herd of suspects without inviting Inspector Cramer, so I called Moira Menzies. She said my idea sounded crazy, but agreed to watch me make a fool of myself.

All I needed were enough chairs in my office to accommodate the guests. Junior Huskey took care of that for me.

* * * *

She may have thought me crazy, but Moira showed up first the next morning. Just to demonstrate she had her own hired muscle, she asked her senior investigator, Cletus Dunn, to tag along.

Moira dressed for the occasion, wearing the police-car-blue suit she saves for big case summations. She looked attractive and professional. Dark blue goes well with her blonde hair, and two inches of lovely knee showed beneath the skirt.

Moments later, Vern Hobbs ushered in the Butterbaugh delegation. I directed Cassie to the comfortable guest chair closest to my desk. It was my show; I wanted the best scenery right up front.

I put Tammy next to Cassie. She, too, looked nice, but I'd yet to see her smile.

R. Wade and Brack Clemons came dressed in suits some Italian designer would have overcharged for. I put them in the second row, behind their womenfolk. R. Wade grunted a hello, while Clemons gave me a big smile and a handshake.

At ten sharp, Joe Costello led in Linda Beets. Melvin and Delphine followed them, and finally Billy Joe Carpenter walked in and took the last seat on my right.

After surveying the scene, I felt an uncontrollable urge to ring for my butler and cook, Fritz Brenner, and ask for two bottles of Reimers beer. That being impossible, I signaled for Junior Huskey to close my office door.

Junior came forward and sat alongside my desk, while Vern Hobbs stood near the door next to Moira.

I went through a round of introductions, saving Ms. Menzies 'til last.

"Now that we know each other," I said, "Let me introduce Ms. Moira Menzies. She represents the District Attorney. The gentleman with her is Investigator Dunn."

Most of the heads swiveled to see the two official guests.

Melvin decided to break the ice. "Jest what in the hell is this all about, Chief?"

"It's about helping me find a killer, Mr. Kite. I've invited you all here to ask questions and get truthful answers."

I remained standing to gain a slight psychological advantage over my audience and tried to look serious.

"Your time is valuable, and so is mine," I said. "If we can limit our conversation to my questions and your answers, I'll be brief."

Melvin mumbled something to Delphine, scowled and looked unhappy.

I sat, took a moment to get comfortable and began my act.

"If I may begin with a brief statement," I said, "Scotty Beets was murdered. My investigation leads me to believe someone in this room killed him."

R. Wade whispered in Clemons' ear. Linda Beets did the same with Joe Costello. Tammy, Melvin, and Delphine made faces. Cassie looked at me and smiled.

"Let's start with what I learned about Mr. Beets. In addition to being a well-respected builder, he recently volunteered to testify against R. Wade Butterbaugh, offering valuable information to local and federal prosecutors."

I looked straight at Butterbaugh.

"That, sir, gives you motive. No Scotty, no damning testimony."

"Bull-shit!" said R. Wade.

Clemons put a calming hand on Butterbaugh's forearm as R. Wade shifted angrily in his chair.

"Chief," Clemons said, "allow me to dispel that myth for ya."

I extended my hand, palm up, indicating he should proceed.

"We've been negotiatin' with the assistant US attorney. Mr. Butterbaugh has agreed ta testify before a Federal grand jury and provide information on the organization responsible not only for smuggling undocumented aliens into the country, but for harboring those people and brokering that labor force ta businessmen all over the US of A. In exchange for his cooperation, Mr. Butterbaugh can expect all charges against him to be conditionally discharged."

Well, that was an unexpected shocker.

"And when was I going to be informed of this?" Moira asked from the back of the room.

"In due time, Miss Menzies. In due time," Clemons said with an oily smile.

"Isn't your client's safety in jeopardy, Mr. Clemons?" I asked.

"If ya look into your lobby, Chief, you'll see two US marshals. They make Mr. Butterbaugh feel quite secure. After he testifies, he'll be well provided for."

I looked at Vern. He in turn looked into the lobby. He nodded and shifted his ever-present toothpick from one side of his mouth to the other. I assumed two suits were sitting in our reception area.

"Congratulations, Mr. Butterbaugh," I said. "I hope you're happy in your new life."

The Feds would probably set him up with a double-wide in Omaha and get him a job as a greeter in Wal-Mart.

"Moving on then," I continued. "More about Mr. Beets. I learned that he had an eye for the ladies. Although a religious man, very involved with his church for many years, Scotty must have missed that business about not coveting thy neighbor's wife."

Cassie put a hand up to conceal her smirk. The Widow Beets wrinkled up her nose, showing distaste for my irreverence.

"We know Mr. Beets had an affair with Cassie Butterbaugh. We also know Mrs. Beets became privy to this information. Pardon the sexist remark, but a woman scorned has historically been a powerful suspect."

It was Joe Costello's turn to speak. "Sam, Mrs. Beets has a solid alibi for the night her late husband spent at the construction site. And before you mention the possibility of hiring someone to kill him, forget it. We'll open all her financial records for you to look at—no large withdrawals to pay a hit man. She'll also take a polygraph exam to establish her innocence."

"Thank you, Counselor. Always a pleasure doing business with you."

Okay, Mrs. Beets, don't sit there so holier than thou with your alibi and so smug because you've hired the best attorney in Blount County. Nobody comes into my police station acting like they own it except me. Try this one on for size.

"Some of you may be wondering why I asked Mr. Carpenter to attend our meeting. I wanted him here because he provided me with crucial information about his friend, Scott Beets."

R. Wade Butterbaugh must have gotten antsy after his ambulance-chasing friend got him off the hook.

"Look here, Chief," he said, "you're wastin' our time with all this noise. Either get ta the point or I'm leavin'."

"You're free to go, Mr. Butterball. I have no hold on you," I said.

I glanced toward the back of the room. Moira sat there rolling her eyes. Next to me, Junior hung his head, hiding a laugh. In the front row, Cassie Butterbaugh treated me to another seven-figure smile and shook her head.

"But, sir," I said, "I'd think you'd sit here patiently and wait to see if I accuse your wife of murder. Or do you really care that little for her?"

R. Wade's blood pressure began rising. His face flushed, and he started to stand. Clemons did the hand on the forearm routine again, and his client sat.

Cassie didn't skip a beat. Not only a hot-looking woman, but totally cool.

"Honestly, people," I said. "Interruptions only prolong the inevitable. Back to Mr. Carpenter.

"The other reason he's here is to answer questions about his affair with Linda Beets."

Carpenter hung his head in silence. Linda stood up.

"How dare you?" she said, looking almost as red as Butterbaugh.

"I dare, Mrs. Beets, because it's true. A very simple investigation taught me either you're having an affair with Mr. Carpenter or you were renting him a parking spot on Wednesday nights...when your husband attended church for several hours."

"Sam, is all this necessary?" Costello asked.

"We'll soon find out," I said.

I approached the final scene with most of my audience pissed off at me. The remainder may have wondered how I intended to add them into my equation.

"Now we come to Mr. Kite," I said. "He too had a vested interest in Mr. Beets' court appearance—at a trial where *his* freedom hung in serious jeopardy. After he refused to cooperate with me, I told Mr. Kite I'd push for no plea bargain to misdemeanor theft in satisfaction for all the grand larcenies he committed. I wanted to convict him after trial and see him do felony time. Scott Beets would help me put him in prison."

Melvin's body language left no uncertainty. He would not be contributing to the old police chief's benevolent fund.

"I was led to believe," I continued, "that Mr. Beets thought Melvin would continue to steal copper from the construction sites."

"Or would he?" I said. "Now, I think that was a rouse. I think Scott Beets wanted compensation for his loss. I learned that insurance didn't cover the copper Melvin took.

The audience now looked more interested. Everyone stared directly at me. A few shifted in their chairs. I planned to capitalize on their undivided attention.

"Melvin sold the valuable copper he stole for scrap value, nominally pennies on the dollar. Dollars Scott Beets would spend to replace the pipes and wire necessary to complete the homes he contracted to build.

"So," I began to theorize, "Scott invited Melvin to meet him and offered to taint his testimony if Melvin brought him the copper he needed to complete his jobs. Only Scott didn't care how Melvin obtained that copper—stealing from others was an acceptable option.

"To sweeten the deal, Scott offered another bargaining chip. That's why Ms. Studsill accompanied Melvin that night."

Melvin and Delphine began flashing nervous looks at each other. Moira tilted her head, interested now in information she'd use at trial. Cassie kept on smiling.

"Mr. Beets' eye for the ladies was not limited to one lady at a time," I said. "He engaged in at least one additional fling while seeing Mrs. Butterbaugh. He also carried on an affair with Tammy Davis."

R. Wade leapt back into action, on his feet this time, defending the reputation of his secretary.

"Jest what in the hell does that have ta do with that common construction worker and copper thief? I've heard you malign my wife. Now you're attackin' my secretary. What's your point?"

"I'm getting there, Mr. B. Hold your water. You'll hear the punch line shortly."

Butterbaugh sat. Again red-faced, he mumbled a few more words to his lawyer.

"Before the interruption, I was about to mention that when I conducted background investigations on all the material players in this story, I learned Tammy Davis has a maiden name. It's Studsill. Tammy is Delphine's daughter."

A dull murmur of remarks clouded the room for several moments.

I continued. "Scott Beets offered to end his affair with Tammy as further inducement for Melvin Kite to produce the expensive copper. He also hinted at telling Tammy's husband, Cole Davis, of her infidelity if Melvin didn't come across with that copper."

Melvin had had enough. He shouted, "Y'all're crazy. You're shootin' in the dark. Me an' Delphine weren't nowheres near that job site the night Scotty's killed."

Melvin was correct, I had been shooting in the dark, but my recon by fire got the desired results.

"Wrong, Melvin, old buddy," I said. "That's a lie."

I opened my desk drawer and took out two evidence bags and a few documents.

"You see, Delphine lost this little earring keeper that night." I dangled the plastic bag for everyone to see. "It's just like the one she's wearing on those silver hoops with the French wires."

"You're still crazy. Lotsa women wear them things," Melvin said.

"But do lots of women smoke these skinny brown cigarettes? This stub from the murder scene is the same brand I saw lying on the coffee table in your trailer. And I'll bet the lipstick on this stub matches the lipstick I'd find in her purse or in your bathroom."

Melvin began to speak again. Delphine sat there shaking her head. Tammy sat busily checking the condition of her nail polish.

"Quiet, Melvin," I said. "I've heard enough from you.

"Right now crime scene investigators are photographing the tire treads on Delphine's Mountaineer to match with tire impressions found at the job site.

"A resident spotted a similar SUV in the Blackberry Valley subdivision that night, and the subcontractor gate code you knew was used to gain access there.

"When the investigators are finished with her car," I picked up several documents, "the court order here, allows them to take a sample of her DNA to match with that on the cigarette butt. Officers have already secured your trailer. I'll have it searched for the lipstick, if necessary. These warrants say I can search the premises and her person."

Delphine extended her hands, palms up. She conceded defeat.

"When Scott suggested Melvin continue to engage in illegal conduct," I said, "conduct he'd already been arrested for, Melvin resented being backed into a corner. He lashed out at his former employer, the man now applying the pressure.

"As they say, folks, the jig is up. You're both under arrest for the murder of Scott Beets. You could invoke your right to remain silent and go away together as killers acting in concert. But if anyone wants to claim the other killed Beets, now's the time to speak."

"I didn't touch that iron bar," Delphine said, quite willing to throw Melvin to the wolves. "Check for fingerprints. Was him who done the killin'. He dropped him down that hole, too."

"Thank you, Ms. Studsill. I'm sure Investigator Dunn will be happy to take your statement.

"Officer Huskey, Officer Hobbs, please remove the prisoners, and lock them up."

Most everyone jumped to their feet. A hum of conversation filled the room. Clete Dunn followed Junior and Vernon. Moira walked up to my desk.

Linda Beets turned first and stormed out. Joe Costello looked at me, smiled and ran his right index finger over his left several times—every parent's signal for 'shame, shame'. R. Wade, Tammy and Clemons followed Billy Joe Carpenter to the lobby.

Cassie stood slowly. "Sugar," she said, "I just loved watchin' you work. That was as good as any movie I've ever seen. Y'all take care

125

now." She waved by wiggling her fingers, turned and walked out…with a bit more wiggle.

After Cassie left, Moira made a face and said, "Y'all take care now." Then she continued. "Lord have mercy, Sam. Was Rex Stout your daddy?"

Moira loves it when I answer one of her snotty remarks with something equally caustic. I think she loves it. Maybe she hates it. It's hard to tell.

"Do you wear those short skirts to influence male jurors?" I asked her.

She gave me the look little girls save for boys who stick their pigtails in an ink well. "Do you always make eyes at your murder suspects?"

I laughed. Lawyers are rarely at a loss for words.

Vern and Junior returned to my office. Vern interrupted the adolescent conversation Moira and I were having.

"Melvin's in a cell a'waitin' fer ya. Clete's gettin' a statement from the woman. I reckon we're about done here."

"Good job, boss," Junior said. "That was jest like on TV."

"I still have one question," I said. "How did Scotty Beets, a skinny little guy with a bad haircut, get all those good-looking women?"

Moira chuckled and turned away from me.

"You know Vernon," she said, flashing her prettiest smile, "I haven't seen you in ages. Walk me out to my car, will you?"

Junior and I looked at each other. I thought Moira just got me again.

THE END

By the Horns of a Cow

Wayne Zurl

By the Horns of a Cow
Wayne Zurl

Somewhere in my town, someone was dragging a really big cow behind his pickup truck. That didn't make me happy.

"How the hell can someone steal a fourteen-foot, brown and white cow and not be seen?" I asked.

"Beats me, boss. If I had time to get into this I wouldn't have called you," Sergeant Stan Rose said. "After midnight we go on overtime, and that doesn't make the mayor happy."

"Where's Mr. Patel now? He owned the cow, didn't he?"

"Not exactly. When he remodeled the store and advertised his grand re-opening, the dairy sent the cow here to draw attention to the business."

"They sent the cow? It travels alone?"

"Don't break my chops, boss. They hauled the cow here with a truck. You must have seen it somewhere before. It's on wheels and has a trailer hitch."

"And the dairy just left it here, unlocked and unattended? Anyone could back up a truck, set the hitch on their ball and drive away with a fourteen-foot Jersey cow in tow?"

"Yep, that's about it," he said.

"And now we've got to find it." I really didn't sound happy, even to myself.

"Isn't our motto *to protect and serve*? I guess this comes under the broad category of serving."

I nodded and scratched my head, not having a clue why I should care.

"It must be pretty hard to hide a fourteen-foot cow," I said.

"If it was me, I'd put it on my front lawn so my neighbors could see it."

"Yeah, but that's you," I said. "You'd probably buy one for your lawn if they sold them."

"I'd rather have a dozen pink flamingoes."

"Sure you would. Where's Patel now?"

"He's home. Won't open the store again until seven o'clock tomorrow morning. He's waiting for you."

"I'm too old for this, Stanley."

"I know, boss. Sorry to call you out. I just thought…"

"Where's he live?"

Stan gave me Sanjeev Patel's address. Patel owned and operated the Git-N-Go market and gas station in Prospect, Tennessee.

With the nearest supermarket twelve miles away in Maryville, Patel's store became the place most everyone in town shopped for their small grocery orders.

You wouldn't have to know much about East Tennessee to infer that Sanjeev Patel wasn't a native of Southern Appalachia. Originally, he came from Madras, India.

I'm not a Tennessee native either. I'm from New York. Stan Rose—he's from Los Angeles. Stanley and I share one thing in common; we're cops for the city of Prospect. I'm the chief, and he's the road sergeant on the four-to-midnight shift.

At 11:45 on a Tuesday night—three quarters of an hour after Patel closed his store, we stood in the Git-N-Go parking lot staring at the empty spot where the big cow once stood. Twenty minutes earlier, Stanley called me about the larceny of that fourteen-foot-tall, trailer-mounted mascot from Richfield Dairies of Philadelphia, Tennessee.

I was tired. Most middle-aged men are tired at 11:45 p.m. after they've worked a full day. I felt a little extra drowsy that night because for dinner my wife Kate and I made a crabmeat casserole with chopped artichoke hearts and fresh mushrooms in a Parmesan white sauce with sherry. And we drank a bottle of Sauvignon Blanc with it. For dessert, I sipped one of my St. Patrick's Day favorites, Bailey's Irish Cream and vodka on the rocks. More in the mood to snuggle up with my good-looking wife than play detective and find an oversized cow, I had less than a positive attitude. But that night Prospect paid me to locate the mammoth bovine. So I played detective.

* * * *

After a few minutes of questioning, I learned neither Mr. Patel nor his twenty-year-old son, Narang, a full-time college student who worked in the store after classes, could offer any leads. Neither saw anyone hanging around the store or the cow before closing.

During the days prior to the theft, no one noticed a customer with an abnormal fondness for king-sized cows. In short, I got bupkis from the proprietors.

Actually, I got much more than that. Mrs. Patel had made chicken korma for dinner and warmed up the leftovers for me. With a piece of Nan bread, mango pickle and a cup of spiced tea, I enjoyed a great midnight snack.

* * * *

At twenty-after-nine the next morning, I walked into Prospect PD. I still felt tired, not in the mood to track down cattle rustlers and certainly not ready to see the mayor who had already left a message with Sergeant Bettye Lambert, asking me to pay him a visit when I arrived.

"Sammy, I know you're a big fan of those old TV westerns, but I never thought you'd have to go out and find any stolen cattle," Bettye said without much luck hiding her amusement.

"It's a good thing I like you or I'd get upset when you make fun of me."

"You'd never get mad at me, would you, darlin'?"

"Is my wife teaching you how to handle me when I'm not happy with the world?"

"You need to go upstairs now, Sammy, and see the mayor. He called down lookin' for ya fifteen minutes ago."

"Yeah, yeah, yeah."

"When you get back I'll have coffee for ya. And I stopped at Richie Creamie on the way in and bought you a jelly doughnut."

"Betts, thank you. You're the only reason I come here in the morning."

"I'll do everything I can to take care of you, Sammy. You know that. Now I need you to go upstairs, and see the mayor. Please."

I grunted something positive about Bettye and negative about the mayor.

* * * *

"I hear y'all worked late last night, Sam. What time'd ya git home?" Mayor Ronnie Shields asked.

We sat in his office, he behind a desk roughly the size of the flight deck of the USS Ronald Reagan, and me in a comfortable, forest green leather chair that must have cost the citizens of Prospect a bundle.

"I walked in a little after one. A fat lot of good the night out did me. I have to start from scratch again today," I said, showing a liberal dose of disgust.

Ronnie smiled. I suppose he wanted to make me forget I worked overtime without compensation. He's a politician; he smiles a lot.

"I got a call from Sonny Richfield early this mornin'," he said. "Seems our Mr. Patel called him late last night."

Sonny Richfield, president of Richfield Dairies and father of the cow, was a well-known figure in East Tennessee. The TV commercials showing him extolling the virtues of his ice cream and the other dairy products his family has produced for generations were traditional media events.

"Sonny says he's prepared to do whatever it takes to recover his cow," Ronnie told me. "He'll hire private detectives, pay a ransom, offer a reward for information—y'all name it. Whatever it takes."

"Has he received a ransom demand?" I asked.

"Didn't say so."

"Well, before he mobilizes an army of Pinkertons or advertises a reward, how about letting me see what I can find out? Once a reward is posted, all the kooks and weirdoes in the tri-state area will call in with cow sightings between here and Chattanooga. You can expect reports of Elvis riding the damn thing up and down I-75."

"I told Sonny there wasn't a better detective in the whole state ta be workin' on the case," Ronnie said, unaffected by my sarcasm. "Sam, you know how proud we are ta have ya workin' in Prospect."

"Thanks, Ron. I'm genuinely overwhelmed. Now I'd better get down to tracking these rustlers." I stood up. "See ya later, trail boss."

* * * *

"You look tired," Bettye said when I got back downstairs. "Your eyes are bloodshot. Did you get any sleep last night?"

I love it when she's concerned about me.

"I slept long enough," I said. "It's allergies. I've had a pollen headache for three days."

"Can't you take medication?"

"Nothing is working this time. If I take a prescription thing before the allergy attack, it prevents headaches. If I get a headache first, it won't relieve it."

"Then why don't you take the medicine each day durin' allergy season?"

"I don't like to take medicine."

"Sam, darlin'…what am I gonna do with you?" She gave me a motherly look.

"Don't say it. I know. Kate's already told me. I anticipate every woman I know will tell me the same thing when they see my eyes watering and hear me sniffle. It must be a maternal thing. Be nice to me, Betts. Don't nag."

"Sure, Sammy. You need anythin' you just let me know."

"I need a fourteen-foot cow—pronto."

"Can't help you there, darlin'."

I had a problem believing this huge cow could disappear with no one seeing it dragged down the road. Git-N-Go closed at 11p.m. Between closing and 11:15 the cow disappeared.

At 11p.m., everything in Prospect is closed except Howell's Pub, which closes at midnight. At 11a.m. when the pub opened for lunch, I'd go there and look for witnesses…or rustlers.

Ten minutes after we last spoke, Bettye walked into my office.

"Seems last night was our time for strange happenings," she said. "I just sent Bobby Crockett to Prospect Hardware. They had a burglary last night. The only things taken were three cases of gold-leaf spray paint. Now how about that?"

"Great. Cattle rustlers and graffiti artists. What next? Tell Bobby to stop by when he's finished there. I've got to make a call before I go to the hardware store."

I needed to contact a lot of people in a short time to see if a witness to the cow-napping lurked somewhere in the woodwork.

Thieves rarely respect territorial boundaries after they steal something. Almost twelve hours had passed since the theft, and the cow could be miles from beautiful downtown Prospect.

Officially, I'd put out an alarm to the surrounding police jurisdictions. That would get me two things—laughs from the cops who read the alarm and possibly some help if a cop stumbled over the big cow while on patrol.

But for maximum efficiency I needed the eyes of the entire population in the Smoky Mountain region on the lookout for Bossie.

I called a friend's cell phone number in Knoxville. A sleepy voice answered.

"Hi, Sam. How are you?" she said.

"How did you know it was me?"

"You're calling from your desk, right?"

"Uh-huh."

I was sitting behind my desk, which is considerably smaller then the mayor's. As Rachel Williamson, a TV reporter, and I spoke, I watched a ladybug walking across my blotter.

"That shows up on my caller ID," she said. "Remember I explained caller ID to you once? Your cell phone doesn't register an ID, but your landline does. Easy, isn't it?"

"I hate technology. I can't be expected to remember things like that. You sound sleepy…did I wake you?"

"I am sleepy, but the clock rang fifteen minutes ago. I've just been lying here waiting for enough energy to get up."

"You're still in bed? What time did you get home last night?"

"12:30…same as every night."

"You finish your show at 11:30. I worked last night until after two o'clock and got to work at seven this morning." I lied. "You've got some life—rich, beautiful and lazy."

"I wish I were rich. If you saw me in the morning without makeup you might not think I'm beautiful, but I love being lazy."

The ladybug tried to walk up the side of my phone, but had trouble with the slippery plastic.

"If you're still in bed, tell me what you're wearing," I said.

"Not a chance, buddy. You'll never know unless you come here and see for yourself."

"Rachel, sweetie, you're like Guinevere tempting Lancelot. That's not fair. You know I can't come there, but you could send a picture."

"It's too early for you to be drinking, so you must be crazy."

We have conversations like that often.

"Let's get down to business," she said. "What's up?"

"Two things, my love, first, stop wearing that white, cable-knit sweater you had on the night before last. That thing is really…uh…form-fitting. I spent the whole half hour looking at you and can't remember the news."

"Oh really? You watch my show and remember what I wear?"

"Of course. You think I care what's happening in the world?" I changed the subject before I got into trouble. "Next thing, can you get something on the noon broadcast for me? Important po-leece stuff."

"Sure…well, I guess…maybe. What's so important?"

"The Richfield cow was stolen last night."

For a moment, I heard nothing but silence, and then she a stifled laugh.

"You're kidding?" she asked. I didn't answer. "You're not, are you?"

I slid a sheet of paper under the ladybug and let her walk onto it. She started her trek across the eight-and-a half-inches of white bond.

"No, I'm not kidding. Someone swiped the big cow from Patel's market in Prospect."

After that simple explanation, she didn't try to muffle her laugh. I tried to picture her. The little dimple in her chin gets accentuated when she laughs. She's very pretty.

"Go ahead…laugh. Make fun of me, and I'll call one of those young hotties on a different channel and ask for help."

"No, you won't," she said, still giggling.

"You're right, I won't. But you shouldn't take me for granted."

"Sam, I'd never do that. You're my best friend, and…well, you know."

"Good, and I do know. I feel the same. But listen," I said. "I need an all-encompassing broadcast asking for everyone's help. Somebody must have seen that poor cow being dragged away. I just hope she doesn't end up chopped meat before I can get her back."

"Sam, this is not a real cow."

"You're sure?"

"Don't be stupid. Okay, I'll call the station and have them put out an appeal," she giggled again, "for information and give your phone number." I heard more snickering. "Then at six o'clock I'll do more story for you. We must have some stock footage or a still shot of that cow somewhere. But you listen to me, mister. If you find that cow and Richfield gives you a reward, I want half of it."

After the ladybug walked for about six inches, I flicked my finger on the bottom of the page. She took flight, heading for the wall ten feet away.

"Yeah, yeah," I said. "I'll get you a reward if you use it to buy us two tickets to Hawaii. Then you'd have to tell your kids you're fooling around with their Uncle Sam."

"You want to fool around in Hawaii?" She sounded interested.

"If we went to Hawaii, I'd take it very seriously."

"Oh, God, you're so sweet. What a smoothie."

"Yeah, and I'm devilishly handsome, too."

"I've always said that. Don't worry, Sammy. I'll take care of you."

"Thanks, kiddo. I owe you again."

"Yes, sir, you sure do."

Rachel Williamson is the senior anchorperson of East Tennessee's most popular news show. With her help, someone might phone in a tip that could lead me to the boosted bovine.

* * * *

Officer Bobby John Crockett rapped his knuckles on the jamb of my office door. I waved him in, and he handed me the burglary report from the hardware store. I learned it had been a simple back door break-in. The door showed jimmy marks near the lock, with a sledgehammer and pry bar most likely used to open and irreparably damage the metal door.

The owner admitted that with so little crime in Prospect he sometimes forgets to set the alarm. It had been one of those nights.

As Bettye told me, the only missing items were three cases—seventy-two spray cans—of gold paint. The cash and coin left in the register overnight—only $98.00—had not been touched. A large inventory of high-ticket power tools also remained there unmolested. That sounded almost as strange as the curious case of the Richfield cow.

I paid a visit to Prospect Hardware for nothing more than public relations value, learning no more than what already appeared in Crockett's report. As I arrived, a handyman worked feverishly replacing the back door. Ervil Boggs, the business owner, swore he'd be more diligent in the future with his alarm. The barn would be locked now that the horse had been stolen, so to speak.

From the hardware store, I drove to Howell's Pub. I looked at my watch. Only 11:05, but I was hungry, ready for lunch as well as ready to continue my investigation.

The manager of the pub, an Englishman named Reggie Smethurst, would have already opened the place. When I arrived, I gave my lunch order to a waitress named Dossie and wandered through the dining area to the pub at the back of the restaurant.

Reggie poured me a pint of black and tan while I sat on a stool at the bar. We exchanged pleasantries before I got down to business.

Then Reggie told me he worked from 11a.m. to 7p.m. that week. Howell Watkins, the owner, arrived for the five-to-midnight shift. After explaining my dilemma, Reggie called Howell at home and handed me the phone.

I learned a Tuesday night in Prospect is like a snowy evening in Miami. Few people are out and about. At eleven o'clock, the pub emptied out. Howell, Boyce the cook and the regular night waitress, Edna Sue, played cards for an hour until closing time. I got the names of two people Howell knew were their last customers.

After I hung up, Dossie brought me a hand-pulled, barbeque pork sandwich the size of half a basketball. A dish of homemade coleslaw accompanied it. Detective work can be rewarding if you know where to eat.

Sitting in the pub, sipping my black and tan, I called Information and got phone numbers for the people Howell told me about. The second man I spoke to, Farris Mosley, sounded helpful.

"Yes, sir," he said, "I left Howell's 'tween 10:30 an' quarter ta 'leven. After that, I headed home, but stopped at the Citgo station on Ellejoy Road. Ya know where Patterson Avenue goes north? Well, I's standin' there while my truck's fillin' up. I done used my credit card ta pay so I didn't need ta go inta the store, and I seen this big ol' cow drive by."

"The Richfield cow?"

"Yes, sir, I 'spect so."

"Which way was it going?"

"Well, o' course I cain't say after I lost sight of hit, but when I seen hit, hit was goin' kindly like east. No, I guess that's sorta northeast, ain't hit?

"What kind of vehicle was towing the cow?"

"The ve-hickle? Hmm. Well, hit was white. Yes, sir—a white dooly, heading northeast on Ellejoy Road.

"Do you remember any more? Was it a Ford, a Chevy, a Dodge? Anything else that would be helpful?"

"Cain't say as I can. I wasn't lookin' as much at the ve-hickle as I's lookin' at the cow. Hit's a big'un, ya know. Oh, one thing I do remember—this ve-hickle had mud flaps with chrome nekked girls on them. Yes, sir, nekked girls."

"Farris, I really thank you. You were a big help."

"Yes, sir. Glad ta he'p ya. Call me anytime. Y'all take care now."

So I made some progress. Not a lot, but progress none the less.

The cow had been rustled by a person or persons unknown driving a white, heavy-duty pickup with dual rear wheels, and chrome, naked girls on the mud flaps. There could only be a few hundred of those wide-assed doolies running around the Smokies, and those mud flaps were only available in every stinking truck stop and truck shop in the country.

But I still felt good about myself. I had obtained information using good old-fashioned police work.

At a loss for anything else to do, I drove back to the PD and asked Bettye to alert all three Prospect cars and then amend the alarm she sent out earlier. Perhaps someone would get lucky and see a white truck with *nekked* girls on the mud flaps.

At one p.m., Bettye went to lunch, and I sat at her desk answering the phones and dispatching the sector cars. At 1:30, I received an interesting call.

"You the head-man there?" a real down-home voice asked me.

"I'm the police chief. Can I help you?"

"I seen that tall, young feller on the TV news t'day at lunch time a'sayin' you's lookin' fer that big cow. That right?"

"Yeah, the cow was stolen from a market in Prospect last night. You know something about that?"

"Mebbe. What's it worth ta ya?"

"You want money for information?"

"O' course. Ain't worth my while ta tell ya fer nothin'."

I just love all our civic-minded citizens.

"The man who owns the cow says he'll pay for information that leads me to find it. I could probably get you a couple hundred dollars."

"I want a thousand dollar."

"Yeah, right. People don't give a thousand dollars to get their kids back. This guy won't pay a grand for a statue of a cow."

"How much ya' give?"

"I said a couple hundred, but I've got to find this cow based on what you tell me. No money for bullshit."

"This ain't no bull-shit. I seen the cow bein' towed, and I seen where they's takin' it."

"Okay, what are we talking about here?"

"Will you give five hunnert afta ya' find the cow?"

"I might get you five hundred, but only after I find the cow and no bullshit."

"I hear that. How's I gonna know y'all find it, and how do I know I'll git paid?"

"If I find the cow you'll hear it again on the news—same channel, maybe at noon, maybe at six o'clock. After you hear that the cow is back, call me again. We'll meet, and I'll bring you the money. You want to stay anonymous?"

"Ain't nobody needs ta know who tol' ya this. And I want cash money—no check. How do I know I kin trust ya?"

"You've got to take my word. If I stiff you, call the mayor. Call the guy who runs the dairy. I'm not going to cheat you out of someone else's five hundred bucks."

"Okay, I'll trust ya."

"First tell me what kind of vehicle you saw towing this cow."

"Big white Dodge 3500 dooly, four by four."

"Okay, that sounds about right. Where's the cow?"

"You know the Prospect Air Park?"

"Yeah, I know where it is."

"Well, ya go jest past the driveway some, then ya turn left onta the gravel road there. It goes inta the woods and up the li'l hill till the road levels out. There's a clearin' up there. Not long ago they's people who grew mary-wanna in that clearin'. Them black helicopters found the crop and put a stop ta that. Before ya git ta the big clearin', look fer a dirt road on the right. Take it ta anotha li'l clearin' where they used ta have a still, but don't no more. The cow's in there."

"Okay, I'll look there today. You know who took it there?"

"I cain't say. Look fer that white dooly."

"You have a name I can call you?"

"You ain't got ta have no name."

"No, I don't, but thanks for the information. It may take a couple of days, but call me when you hear something on the television.

"I'll call ya." He hung up.

A few minutes later Bettye came back from lunch.

"Betts, I'm the greatest detective since Sherlock Holmes. I feel better now. I lost my headache, and I took a phone call from someone who says the cow's out by the air park. Call Vern Hobbs and have him meet me at the office there. Call the mayor, and have him call Sonny Richfield. It'll cost Sonny five hundred bucks to get his cow back. *Cash money. No check.* After I find the cow, he has to come up with the dough. I gotta go. Call Vern. See ya later. Oh, by the way, who owns the air park?"

Bettye clicked a couple of keys on the computer and tapped in the business name.

"Our records show a C.A. Goodhardt, LTC (retired) as the owner.

You know what that means?"

"Lieutenant Colonel, retired. Probably an ex-flyer with his own little airport for amusement. Something like me—an ex-cop with my own amusing little PD."

"Maybe you two can tell jokes and amuse each other."

"Aren't we just so humorous today, Sergeant?"

"Bye, Sammy." She made the first word sound like something a sheep says.

* * * *

I drove for fifteen minutes to find the airfield in a sparsely populated section of Prospect, almost bordering the community of Seymour in adjoining Sevier County.

The country roads took me through hilly pastures where small herds of cattle grazed or horses walked around nibbling the grass. The soil there wasn't much good for farming so the few level areas of the valley became home for a couple of churches, an RV resort and the Prospect Air Park.

I pulled into the gravel lot and parked in front of a single story, pre-fab building. The sign said Prospect Aviation and Air Park, C.A Goodhardt and A.A. Goodhardt, owners.

I took the three steps up and opened the door. A business counter blocked access to the larger room behind it. To the right of the door a waiting area with several chairs against the wall, a table and folding chairs in the center of the room, and soda and snack machines on another wall, would accommodate serious customers. Two desks sat behind the counter to the left.

The administration building conspicuously lacked any people. I walked through and out the back door toward the grass runway. A two-story, corrugated metal hangar sat at an angle to the road; the tall sliding doors were open. Parked inside the hangar, an old, red biplane faced the landing strip.

A half-dozen small planes sat on the verge of the runway, guy wires securing them to the ground. I walked into the hangar, stood on the port side of the biplane and admired the shiny paint and classic lines. Just as attractive was the female backside, covered by an Air Force-gray flight suit that swayed slightly left and then right while the upper portion of the attached body worked inside the hull.

"Pardon me?" I said.

"Hold your horses. I've got to connect this cable, and I'm having a hard time with it. It's tough to see in here. Ha! There ya go. Got it."

She withdrew her shoulders from the trapdoor, stood upright and turned around. I saw Prospect Aviation embroidered on the left breast of her flight suit. The owner of that shapely backside qualified as the best-looking aviation mechanic I'd ever seen. She looked to be in her late thirties, had her dark hair pulled back in a ponytail, with medium-length bangs crossing her forehead. A grease smudge marked her left cheek, and she held a crescent wrench loosely in her right hand.

"Hi, can I help you?" she asked, in a voice lacking a Tennessee accent.

"I hope so." I showed her my badge. "My name's Sam Jenkins. I'm with the Prospect Police. Would you have a minute to answer a few questions?"

"What's that say on the badge?" she asked, "Come closer. I need glasses and can't wear my contacts when I work on the plane."

We both took a step toward each other. She squinted at the large silver and gold oval shield I held. I smiled at her.

"I thought you might be the new chief. You are as cute as they say."

"Thanks. Who are *they*?"

"A couple of my friends saw you on TV once. They said you were cute, but you'd look younger without the gray hair."

I chuckled at her honesty. "Do you mean I should shave my head or color my hair?"

She laughed. "No, don't shave your head. I think the gray looks good, kind of distinguished maybe." She looked closely at my face. "Do you know your left eye is watering? You have a cold or something?"

I shook my head. "Allergies. Too much pollen around."

"You should take medication."

"So I've been told."

"You wanted to ask me questions?"

"Yeah, are you C.A. Goodhardt?"

"No, that's my father. I'm A.A.—Amelia Ann Goodhardt. Dad's in

Charleston for a week."

"Are you a pilot, too?"

"Have been since I was a kid. I'm an Air Force brat. When Dad was stationed up in Alaska, he taught me how to fly. Kids up there learn at eleven or twelve. You fly before you get a driver's license."

"The Red Baron here yours?"

She beamed proudly. "Yeah. You like her?"

"Cool—like in *High Road to China.*"

"Yeah, yeah. I love that movie."

"Me, too," I said.

"Wanna go for a ride?" She sounded enthusiastic.

"Sure, but right now I've got to act like a cop. I'm doing an investigation that's getting a few laughs from whomever I talk to about it. I'm looking for…"

She cut me short with another laugh. "I know—the Richfield cow. Heard about it on the news. That is pretty funny."

I shrugged. "Yeah, I guess. I received a phone call today from a guy saying I could find the cow in the woods near here. Can we take a walk outside for a minute?"

We did. The blue sky didn't have a cloud in it. It would have been a fine day for open-cockpit flying.

"From the description I have, I think the cow may be in the woods off the road over there." I pointed to a narrow gravel road at the base of a rise several hundred yards behind the runway. "I see the road from here. How do I find where it connects to the blacktop?"

She gave her head a quick shake, and her ponytail swung from side to side. "That's not exactly easy. You have to go another quarter mile or more and run over a right-of-way between two fields. A couple hundred yards further up, it widens and has a gravel top. The best way to get there is across the runway, over that rough patch and then onto the gravel. What are you driving?"

"A big Ford."

She shook her head. "You'd need more ground clearance in the rough. Come on, jump in my Jeep, and I'll take you."

A tan Wrangler sat in the sun, parked next to the hanger. We drove over the smooth, grass runway. Swallows zigzagged in flight across the

143

field, dog-fighting with the insects Amelia's Jeep disturbed as we crossed the grass.

Leaving the smooth runway, we bounced over the two hundred yards of uneven ground before we reached the gravel and the base of the hill. Another quarter mile angling upward and we entered a tree line on a level plateau situated fifty or more feet above the valley floor.

Amelia slowed down and drove on the gravel at barely ten miles an hour. The road narrowed again. Trees grew to the edge of the gravel, and their tops spread over the road, interlocking and creating a thick canopy.

"There's a big clearing up ahead where some local boys grew pot until DEA spotted it and busted them," she said. "There are a couple of trails off this road before you get to that clearing. Lover's lanes mostly, but there is one wide enough to get in and turn a trailer around. It's the only place to hide your cow without being seen from the air. Let's try it."

"You're the pilot."

I guess she liked that observation. She turned and smiled at me.

We crept along the gravel until a dirt road appeared on the right. She turned in. A hundred yards up the trail, a freshly cut cedar blocked our path.

"Now, that's a good sign," I said, "but inconvenient as hell. I'll see if I can swing it off the road."

"If it's too heavy, I've got a towrope," she said. "We can use the Jeep and pull it to the side."

I grabbed the still green tree by the top and with a little effort swung it parallel to the road, leaving just enough room for the Jeep to pass.

I opened the passenger door and told Amelia, "I'll walk ahead in case they have a trip wire or something that would tell them someone found their hiding place—assuming this is their hiding place. Follow me. If I hold up my arm, stop."

"You're a real soldier, aren't you?"

"We'll see. If I fall over a wire and make an ass of myself, you'll have your answer."

We traveled less than another hundred yards and encountered no new obstacles to discourage us. I stopped and stood there. Amelia stopped the Jeep, got out, and came to stand next to me. In a tree-rimmed clearing facing us stood my missing cow. Eighty-percent of it now painted gold.

"Damn, that thing looks big," Amelia said.

"Fourteen feet plus the wheels."

"Damn."

"We've just solved the Prospect Hardware Store burglary, too. Last night three cases of gold spray-paint were stolen from there."

"Convenient."

"Now I have to catch the cow-nappers."

"Can't be all that tough."

"Just need a plan."

"I guess."

"Why paint it gold?" I asked.

"Sounds almost mythological or Biblical or something."

"I think golden sheep were more popular back then."

"You sure?"

"No."

"You have a plan?"

"Not yet."

"I've only known you for fifteen minutes, but I bet you'll make one."

"I guess."

"Wanna go back?" she asked.

"Sure, can't stay here. Stop at the cedar. I'll block the trail again."

"Okay."

When we got back to the airpark, Amelia drove to the admin building. We entered through the back door and found Vern Hobbs sitting at the table drinking a can of Mountain Dew.

"Hey, boss," he said and stood.

"Amelia, this is Vernon Hobbs. Vern, Amelia Goodhardt."

Amelia stood a couple of inches taller than Vern who I thought was the world's shortest cop.

"Howdy, ma'am." Vern extended his hand.

"Hello, Vern."

They shook hands.

"Wanna buy a cow, Vern?" I asked.

"You find it already?"

I nodded. "With Ms. Goodhardt's help."

"Shoot," he said.

"Now we have to keep an eye on the spot until the rustlers come back to fetch her. Hang out here until I send someone with an unmarked four-by-four. I'll drive your car back to town. You keep my Ford here. You have a jacket to wear over your uniform?"

"Yessir, shore do."

"Amelia, will you show Vernon where to sit and watch the trail?

"Sure…Sam. I'd be happy to."

I looked at Vern. "It's most likely we're looking for a big white Dodge pickup with dual wheels. I've got a pair of binoculars in my car."

Amelia turned to me. "Is there anything else I can do for you? Any way I can help?"

"If you don't mind us hanging around your airfield for a while, that would be a big help. I'll get a couple of guys to sit up in the woods. I'd like to come back later today and hang out here. I'll watch the road and give the guys in the woods a heads-up if I see the white truck heading toward them."

"Sure. Do you mind if I keep you company? This is exciting."

"You can tell me about your biplane. You'll keep me from falling asleep."

"Oh, I can do that."

"Okay, I'll see you guys later. Vern, come on outside, and we'll swap cars."

In the parking lot Vern told me, "Gat dag, she's a purty one, ain't she?"

"Sure is, partner."

"Dag, she's purty." Vern sounded impressed.

"Steady, Pops. Guys our age can't be getting excited too often."

"I ain't as old as you."

"Thanks." I always appreciate hearing things like that.

* * * *

"Miss Bettye, who do you think just found the giant cow?" I asked.

"Lord have mercy, who could it be?"

"Don't toy with my emotions, school marm. You know damn well

I'm the only gunslinger here in Tombstone who could find a rustled cow."

"Oh, Sammy, I'm jest as happy as a 'possum settin' in a per-simmon tree."

"Wow."

"I just knew you could do it, Mr. Dillon." She started giggling.

I guess everybody watches *Gunsmoke* reruns.

"Go ahead, and laugh. When I write my memoirs, I won't give you any credit when I tell the adventure of the giant cow."

"Oh, yes, you will."

"And people wonder why men become misogynists."

"I'll bet you think I don't know what that word means."

"Not true. You're too smart for your own good."

"And you're the last man who could claim to dislike women."

"Ha!"

"What's your plan to catch the rustlers, cowboy?"

"Glad you asked. Call around, and find two volunteers to spend at least one evening in the woods. I'll tell Ronnie all about this and make another call or two."

I called my wife and told her why I wouldn't be home for dinner. My second call went to Rachel telling her that a story was imminent, but I needed her to keep broadcasting a plea for help in finding the Richfield cow. I didn't want the thieves to think we had made any progress.

I changed from sport jacket and khakis to a pair of jeans and a sweatshirt I kept in my PD locker for such occasions. I'd hate to be running through the woods in good clothing.

May in the Smokies can be unpredictable. I've seen days in the low 80s and nights that dip below freezing. The locals are fond of saying, 'If you're not happy with our weather, wait ten minutes, it might could change.' With that in mind, I took my old Army field jacket in case I ended up spending a late night on the airfield waiting for the cow-nappers.

By 4 p.m., I had Vern relieved by two cops driving a four-by-four pickup. They hid themselves and their truck in the woods and waited.

By 4:30, I picked up a sandwich for dinner and pulled into the lot of the airpark. I found the office locked and the hanger doors closed.

Amelia was nowhere in sight.

I took my jacket, binoculars and portable radio transmitter to the side of the hangar and found a spot still covered with afternoon sun. I told my two cops I was in position and would radio a warning if I saw a vehicle driving their way. Then as I'd do on any surveillance, I got comfortable.

In only twenty minutes, something happened. Not along the gravel road, but behind me in the hangar. I heard a small door open. Only seconds later, an attached spring automatically slammed the door shut.

I waited a few moments, listened and then walked around to the front. I found Amelia's Jeep parked there, and I entered the unlocked door. On the left side of the building, not far from where I'd been sitting outside, I watched her unlock the double sliding doors and push them open. Just inside the hanger, she had already set up a folding table and two chairs.

The table, covered with a red and white checked tablecloth, was outfitted with two place settings of china. A large salad bowl occupied the center, a long French baguette and a bottle of white wine sat on either side.

I cleared my throat just to make a little noise. She turned around as I walked over.

"Hi," I said. "I couldn't find you before, so I started waiting outside."

She showed me a guilty smile, like a little girl found using her mother's lipstick. "Oh, you caught me. I just got back, but I guess you know that. After you left, I got out our picnic set. I stopped home for a few minutes and then picked up some things at the store. I thought you might not have an opportunity to eat. I brought you something."

"Yeah, I see. Thanks. Not too many stakeouts get this fancy."

"Actually, I brought *us* something. I hope you don't mind a little company for dinner."

"It's nice having company for dinner. What did you get?"

"Oh, I didn't have time to make anything. I just picked up some pasta and broccoli salad at the deli section and some shrimp, too. I thought they'd go together."

"That sounds great."

It looked like during her stop at home she washed her hair. The ponytail was gone. Her dark brown hair ended a couple of inches below her shoulders and shined in the backlighting that came through the doors. She wore a little make up, a lightweight, navy blue sweater over a white button down blouse, blue jeans and a pair of penny loafers. It would have been physically impossible for the jeans to fit more perfectly; she looked beautiful.

"I never asked, but can you have a glass of wine while you're on duty?" she asked.

"Sure, I could manage that. Unless you asked me to have two then I'd have a second."

That got me another smile. She turned, and the sunlight made her brown eyes sparkle.

"I asked the guy in the liquor store what he had cold that was good. He suggested this. I hope you like it."

"The guy knows his wine. That's a nice chardonnay. I've had it before. Thanks again"

"You're welcome. Ah, anything happening out there?"

"Not so far. I just sat down in the sun trying to stay awake. At my age, it's not always that easy."

"Somehow I don't believe that."

I looked at her for a few seconds, wondering why this attractive woman, young enough to be my daughter, decided to treat me so nicely. Great for my ego, but I hoped things weren't heading somewhere I couldn't sail.

"I'll bet you've had a busy day. Are you hungry?" I asked. She nodded. "Then sit down while I open the wine."

She spent a frantic moment looking through a purse large enough to hold a full set of mechanic's tools. "Oh, damn, I forgot the corkscrew."

"We don't have a problem here. You're looking at an ex-soldier who spent a few of his summer camps in Europe. A pocket knife with a corkscrew was more important than a bayonet over there."

I popped the cork and poured the wine while she served the salad.

Everything tasted wonderful—an excellent spur-of-the-moment meal. Amelia and her comrades in the deli department should have been proud of themselves.

We sat just inside the hanger, out of the sun, but still able to watch the road. I enjoyed the dinner and the company, but I still paid attention to the woods and the case.

By six o'clock, we finished eating, cleaned up the dishes, stowed them back in her office and sat outside again watching the road, sipping our last few ounces of chardonnay. Amelia told me she felt chilly, so I draped my field jacket over her shoulders.

"How long have you worked with your dad?" I asked.

"He retired in '98 after thirty years in the Air Force. He had this place running by 2001. I came here five years ago."

"It sounds like you and dad get along really well."

"He's a great guy. My mom passed away two years ago. I'm glad we had each other. It was hard for both of us."

I expressed my regrets on the death of her mother and thought I better understood why she became interested in an old guy like me. Sure, I'm as cute as the dickens, charming, irresistible to most women and exceedingly modest, but also realistic enough to recognize a parental fixation when I saw one.

I didn't tell her what I thought, needing something witty and entertaining to say, when a white truck kicking up a wake of dust on the gravel road grabbed our attention.

I pressed the key on my radio and gave POs Harlan Flatt and Leonard Alcock a warning of things to come.

I waited several minutes, heard nothing and then called Harley's cell phone, the one he promised to turn to vibrate so we could communicate without the bad guys hearing us.

"What are they doing?" I asked.

"One o' them's paintin' the legs o' the cow. T'other's up on a ladder paintin' some message on the cow's side."

"What?" I said.

Next to me, Amelia heard what Harley said and laughed.

"Boss, y'all heard me. They hooked the cow up ta their truck. I suspect when they's finished they'll be movin' out."

"Harley, tell me this isn't an episode of Candid Camera."

"Do what?"

"Forget it. I'll wait until you call again—when they're on the move."

"10-4, boss."

"Do you guys do stuff like this all the time?" Amelia asked.

"This is my first cow. Usually I take giant cats out of trees for old ladies."

Amelia was one of those women with a great laugh.

I called Sergeant Stan Rose and asked for him and another car to drive up to the airpark. I planned to catch the rustlers on the narrow road as they left the woodland, a spot where they couldn't turn the truck or make a motorized run for it. We continued to wait.

"Too bad I didn't bring another bottle of wine," I said.

"You could drink another bottle of wine and still function? I could close my eyes and go to sleep." She hugged my field jacket around herself like a straight jacket.

"Obviously you don't know any other cops."

"No, you're my first. Is that a good thing?"

"Be my guess."

She laughed again. *I'm as entertaining as a Catskill comic. Don Rickles with a gun.*

At five-to-eight, Stan called my cell phone.

"The dispatcher just told Junior there's a burglary in progress at the Prospect Elementary School. Joey was sent to assist. What do you think?"

"I think it's a false alarm. I think the cattle rustlers are going to move out, and they want our posse to head over to the school marm's place. Sharpen yer spurs, podna, and you two git ready ta ride."

"You know you're nuts, don't you?"

"Is that any way to talk to your fearless leader?"

"I'm ready, fearless leader. You using the portable next?"

"Yeah, hang in there."

Just then, my radio came to life.

"Woods detail to Prospect-one. They jest started up and are movin' out. We're ready."

"10-4, woods detail," I said. "535, you and 509 block the road. No lights until you see them approach. Harley, follow them, but don't let them see your brake lights. I'm going to flank them to their right and be ready if they try to make a run through the rough. If they bail out, you guys be ready to join in the foot pursuit."

I looked over at Amelia.

"Can I come?" she asked.

"Hell yes, woman! You're driving."

We got into her Jeep and without the benefit of lights, drove slowly across the rough meadow toward the gravel road. I heard the big diesel engine of the Dodge before I saw the truck hauling the cow toward Stan Rose and Will Sparks.

We stopped fifteen yards from the gravel in high weeds. I got out and waited. Amelia killed the engine, but stayed ready in case she needed to move quickly.

The next things we saw were the headlights and the flashing blue lights activated on Stan's marked cruiser. I no longer heard the truck tires crunching gravel. Then from behind the cow, another pair of headlights came on. I heard Harley yell, "Police, turn off your engine, and don't move!"

Suddenly two truck doors opened, and I heard someone running toward me. I crouched and waited. As soon as I saw the figure less than five yards away, I hit it with the beam from my four-cell flashlight and fired a shot into the air to get everyone's attention. Warning shots seem more permissible in Tennessee than they ever were in New York.

"Jesus Christ! Don't shoot! Please don't shoot!" my subject cried out.

"On the ground—quick—on the ground!" I yelled, not wanting to give him time to think.

The figure complied. I walked over, my flash light held at arm's length, my revolver still pointed at the subject.

"Christ Almighty, don't shoot me. I give up. Honest, I give up. You kin have the fuckin' cow. Jest don't hurt me."

I squatted down next to my prisoner who already lay face down in the grass. His hands were on top of his head, his fingers interlocked. I turned off the light so my eyes could adjust to the darkness. I holstered my gun, took out my handcuffs and put my knee into the small of his back. Then I smacked him on top of his head.

"Watch your mouth, moron. There's a lady nearby."

"Okay, okay, I didn't know. I'm sorry."

I smacked him again and cuffed him. When I walked my prisoner over to where Stan and the three cops waited, I saw a second man cuffed and in custody. Both thieves stood side by side. I turned my light to illuminate their faces. I looked at Stanley. The other three cops looked at me.

"Son-of-a-bitch!" I said. "They come in matched pairs."

"It must be you," Stan said, looking at me. "I've been on the job for nine years, and I've never gotten into stuff like I get into with you."

"You're just jealous because you can't do things like this on your own," I said.

"I know I'm not a cop," Amelia said, "so forgive me for saying anything, but I remember my father telling me about one of his favorite TV shows—The Twilight Zone. Am I part of an episode right now?"

I addressed the two subjects, "Who are you guys?"

The one wearing a black T-shirt spoke first, "I'm Jeremiah, an' this is my brother Jericho."

"You boys have a last name?" I asked.

In unison they said, "Tisdale."

Jeremiah and Jericho Tisdale were identical twins.

"Okay, everyone remember this. Jeremiah is in the black shirt, and Jericho has the gray one. Boys, if I catch you changing clothes, I'll make your lives miserable. Understand me?"

"Yes, sir," they both answered.

We ironed out the logistics of transporting the prisoners back to the Municipal Building. Amelia and I drove back to the hangar and my car. I helped her close up and thanked her for dinner and the company.

"I had an exciting evening," she said. "Will I see you again?"

"Sure you will. I'll come back to let you know how this plays out. You can introduce me to your dad. Okay?"

"That would be nice." She smiled and kissed me on the cheek. "Don't forget. I'll be waiting."

Why me?

* * * *

We returned to the well-lit municipal parking lot in downtown

Prospect and saw the once brown and white Jersey cow sporting a shiny, new gold paintjob. On one side, in large letters we read the message: "Rebels Rule." On the other side, we were told: "Rebels Rock".

After questioning the Tisdale twins, both recent alumni of Maryville High School, whose nickname is the Rebels, we learned they intended to leave the cow at the gates of their rivals, Heritage High School.

Jericho informed me he had been forced to read parts of the Iliad during his senior year. Bored by much of the saga, but impressed by the story of the Trojan horse, he persuaded his brother to help him leave the gift of a Trojan cow at the gates of their rival school just before the Heritage Mountaineers held their senior prom.

They didn't want to hide inside the statue like a couple of mischievous ancient Greeks, but the Tisdale boys wanted the fourteen-foot cow to imply that while the Maryville Rebels both rock and rule, the Mountaineers were strictly second rate.

Not only were the Tisdales charged with grand larceny for copping the cow, but also with the burglary of the hardware store, and yet another larceny, that of a twenty-four-foot extension ladder from the truck of a local roofer. That crime escaped my attention.

They purchased the last case of gold paint they needed and a few cans of black for the lettering at Wal-Mart. Thanks to the twins, it had been a productive night for Prospect PD.

While Officers Flatt and Alcock processed the Tisdale brothers, I called Rachel Williamson.

"The cow has been rescued. The case is solved."

"Congratulations. Can I buy you an ice cream?" she offered.

"Yes, you can, but first I need an update on the 11 o'clock news. If you send a cameraman down here he can photograph Bossie and—"

She interrupted. "Molly."

"What?"

"Molly—the cow's name is Molly."

"The cow has a name? It's not alive. Why does it need a name?"

"I don't know that it needs a name, but it has one. She's Molly."

"I knew I should have stayed retired."

"You sound congested. Have you been outside a lot today?"

"Sort of."

"Are your allergies bothering you?"

"I'm okay."

"Do you have another headache?"

"Yeah, ah…no. I'm alright. Don't worry about it."

"Sam, you should be taking that medication. Yesterday your voice sounded funny. You know the pollen is bad for you."

"I'm okay, really. No need to treat me like Felix Unger."

"Felix who?"

"Someone before your time. It doesn't matter. Will you send a cameraman to see Molly?"

"Yes. Do you want me to tell everyone Molly is safe now?" She laughed.

"This one is important. I made a deal with the guy who called with information. I said I'd get him five hundred dollars if I found the cow where he told me I would. When he hears you say the cow is home again, he'll call me."

"This is really funny," she said.

"No, it's pathetic."

* * * *

Late the next morning I walked into Ronnie Shields' office. A familiar face smiled at me while the mayor spoke. "Sam, I want y'all to meet Mr. Sonny Richfield. Sonny, this is Sam Jenkins, our police chief. Sam found your Molly and arrested two Murr-vull boys for stealin' the cow and for two other related crimes."

Sonny and I shook hands. He was almost as tall as his cow. Well, not really. Maybe six-five. He had a big happy face and thinning sandy hair. He smiled a lot while I explained my story about buying the information.

"Well o' course, I'll give you the money," Sonny said and beamed with happiness over the return of his pet cow. "I told the mayor here I'd back you anyway I could. You say he wanted a thousand, and you talked him down to five hundred? Well, golly bum, ain't that somethin'? Ya know what, Sam? I'm so happy y'all got Molly back, I'm gonna give the man that whole thousand. How's that?"

No matter how much I tried to explain that this guy was only an informant and even five-hundred represented a big piece of change to pay for a lousy cow, Sonny wouldn't hear me. He gave me ten one-hundred-dollar bills to pay off my tipster. Then I waited for my phone message.

* * * *

The next morning the same man called on the office line.

"You go git the cow yerse'f?"

"I did."

"You git the money?"

"Uh-huh. Got it right here."

"Meet me t'night?"

"Sure. When and where?"

"Same place the cow was. 7:30?"

"Okay," I said. "Wear a carnation in your lapel so I recognize you."

"Do what?"

"Nothing. I'll be there, in the clearing."

"7:30. You park first, an' I'll find ya."

He hung up.

At 7:15, Stan and I sat in my car in the clearing where the cow had been hidden. At 7:30, a solitary man walked down the dirt trail toward us. We got out of the car. The man looked to be in his forties, about five-ten and thin. He wore a green John Deere baseball cap, a plaid flannel shirt and carpenter jeans. He stopped ten feet from the car.

"You walked here?" I asked.

"My truck's parked over yonder." He poked a thumb over his left shoulder. "Who's he?" he asked, nodding toward Stan.

"My son, Stanley."

He made a face. Stan Rose is a six-foot-four-inch black man.

"Listen," I said, "I promised you five hundred."

He began to frown, probably thinking I might stiff him for his money.

"The guy who owns the cow wants to give you the thousand you asked for. It's your lucky day. Thanks for the 4-1-1." I handed him the ten hundred-dollar bills.

"You coulda kept the rest fer yerse'f. How come ya give it ta me?"

"It's not my money," I said. "The owner's happy you helped. He wanted you to have that much."

"I 'preciate that."

"Well, thanks again." I waited for him to leave.

"Y'all didn't have ta give me this here extra cash. I figger I owe you somethin' more."

"Don't worry about it. You earned your money. The dairy owner is happy to get his cow back."

"Nope," he said, "Someday I jest might could do ya another favor. I owe ya that much."

"Okay, then," I said. "Thank you."

"If ya don't mind, I'll leave by myse'f now."

"Sure, we'll hang out here for a couple minutes."

Our informant nodded, turned and disappeared down the trail and into the bushes. We never saw what he drove into the woods and never got a plate number.

I turned to Stanley. "What do you make of that?"

"Beats the hell outta me. And I thought people in LA were different."

* * * *

On Friday morning, I picked up a $25.00 bottle of Russian River Valley chardonnay. At noon, I drove out to the airpark. In the office, a guy about my age sat at one of the desks.

"I guess you're C.A. Goodhardt," I said.

"Yeah, I'm Charlie."

"Hello, Charlie, I'm Sam Jenkins. Your daughter around?"

He looked at me and then at the gift-bagged bottle I carried. "Take a walk out back, and stick around for a minute. You'll see her."

I stood near the runway. A few hundred feet overhead a red biplane twisted, rolled and did a loop. Then it banked to the southeast, turned again and approached the grass strip against the wind. Amelia set the wheels down gently and taxied up to the hangar entrance. I walked over.

She unhooked her harness and climbed down from the cockpit. Once on the ground she took off her goggles and leather flyer's helmet and shook out her hair. She saw me and smiled.

"Hi. What are you doing here?" she asked.

"I wanted to bring you this." I held out the bottle of wine. "As thanks for dinner and your help the other night."

"Oh, you didn't—"

"Yeah, I did. My wife suggested I do it."

"Your wife? Wow, I guess…I didn't see a ring. Wow, I feel really stupid."

"Don't. I can be stupid enough for both of us."

"I guess I should have asked."

"And I should have told you. But neither of us…well, I guess you and your dad can have a drink on me. I hope you both enjoy it."

"I suppose you're not here to take a ride in my plane?"

"Not today. I have to be in court. But I'm sure I'll need a ride some time."

"I don't want you to need a ride. I'd like you to want a ride."

"Whether I need a ride or just want to see the mountains from a plane, I'd want you to be the pilot." I turned to go.

"Hey, Sam," she said, "This thing's gassed up and ready to go. Don't wait too long."

I smiled again, waved and walked back to the admin building.

On my way out, I rapped my knuckles twice on the counter. "Good to meet you Charlie," and headed for the door.

"Hey, have we met before?" he asked.

"I don't think so, but you're probably familiar with my type."

"Amy's been smiling a lot since I got back from Charleston. You the reason for that?"

"I doubt it. I'm so old, I'll bet I'm your age."

He laughed.

"You're not gonna hurt my little girl, are you?"

"You'll have to ask her, but I have no intention to do that. Besides, your kid seems like a tough lady. I'll bet she's a great pilot."

"Yeah, she's both. Maybe I'll see you around."

* * * *

The Tisdale brothers obsessed over the Trojan horse of Greek mythology. Their obsession got them ninety days in the county jail and the bill for Molly's new paint job.

I think they should have spoken to Mr. Patel and learned something from Hindu mythology—how there are some who believe that one should never mess with a heifer, for it is said, "The gates of heaven are opened by the horns of a cow."

THE END

Serpents & Scoundrels
Sequel to
By the Horns of a Cow

Wayne Zurl

Serpents & Scoundrels
—Sequel to By the Horns of a Cow—
Wayne Zurl

When I lived in New York, Tennessee looked like a relatively easygoing place. New York was a refuge for drug dealers, organized crime, carjackers, burglars—you name it. As a cop, I met them all.

I thought the sleepy little town of Prospect would be a milk run for its police chief—me. Well, not exactly.

Sometimes horrible things happen to me while sitting behind my desk at Prospect PD.

For instance…

I sat there initialing reports one Tuesday morning—or was it a Wednesday? I can't remember. What I do recall turned out to be one of the strangest cases I've ever investigated.

My intercom buzzed.

"Yes, dahling," I said. "Is it time for cocktails already?"

Sergeant Bettye Lambert laughed into the phone. "Sammy, you always say somethin' to amaze me. It's ten o'clock in the mornin'. If I drank a cocktail, I'd fall asleep."

"Oh, well, I tried. What's up?"

"Call for you. Won't say who he is. Just said tell you it's the man with the John Deere hat."

"Okay. That narrows it down to only four-hundred-fifty-thousand adult males in the state."

"That's why you get the big bucks, darlin'."

She transferred the call.

"This is Chief Jenkins…may I help you?"

"'Member me?"

163

The accent sounded very local. I wasn't surprised.

"Your voice is familiar. Help me out a little."

"I gave ya the information 'bout the stolen cow. Ya got me that reward money. 'Member now?"

"Sure I do. You wore a John Deere hat when we met you in the woods."

"Yep. 'Member I said I owed ya another favor?"

"I do."

"Okay, this is a good one. Meet me same place as last time…that li'l clearin' back o' the air park."

"Want to give me a hint what it's about?"

"I'll tell ya when we meet up. Ya comin'?"

"Sure. What time?"

"'Bout eight o'clock t'night. Ya bringin' that big black feller with ya?"

"Yeah, he's my partner."

"Okay. See ya then."

He hung up.

* * * *

At 7:45, Sergeant Stanley Rose and I sat in my unmarked Crown Victoria parked in a lonely clearing in the hinterlands of Prospect. Once the hideout of moonshiners, that wooded area changed its economic use from untaxed liquor to a different cash crop until the DEA busted up a lucrative marijuana growing business.

After the pot disappeared, the desolate woodland, connected by makeshift trails, accommodated clandestine lovers and the occasional thief needing privacy. And then it became a place for me to meet informants.

"Wonder what John Deere has this time?" Stan asked.

"He wouldn't say. Likes to play the man of mystery. Who knows? Maybe some old man with a still is back in business."

"Hope the mosquitoes don't find us when we get out of the car."

"You're a born pessimist. Didn't mosquitoes bite you when you were an LAPD cop?"

"Not me."

Stanley is six-four and built like a heavyweight wrestler. Few creatures would dare to bite him.

"I think our boy is heading this way," Stan said.

A solitary figure suddenly appeared on the trail no more than a hundred feet from where we sat. John Deere, as we called him, appeared to be in his forties—medium height and thin build. The bright green and yellow baseball cap sat on his head at a jaunty angle. The rest of his wardrobe consisted of a plaid shirt with the sleeves cut off at the shoulder seams and blue denim overalls.

We got out of the car and met him in the middle of the trail.

"Howdy," I said, trying to embrace the local culture. Stanley nodded to him.

"Whatcha say?" he responded and waited.

"You understand I don't have money to always pay for information."

"I done tol' ya I owed ya one more favor for the extry cash ya got me. Ya coulda kept it yerse'f. We been through that."

"I know."

"Don't know if ya gonna like what I show ya, but it's a good'un. Ya gotta foller me."

"We driving?"

"No, it ain't fer."

He turned and walked down the trail.

Stan and I followed. When we reached the narrow gravel road, he turned right. The daylight had been fading, but even under the forest canopy, enough light filtered through for us to follow him without using our flashlights.

A few minutes' walk put us in a clearing ten times larger than the one we left.

"This here's where they used ta grow the mary-wanna," he said. "Look over yonder at this."

In the upper left corner of the circular clearing, I saw a pile of hastily mounded leaves. We walked closer. Poking out from the bottom of the leaves, I noticed a two-tone brown cowboy boot.

"What the hell?" I said. "Stan, give me some light here."

Both our flashlights probed the pile of leaves. Directly opposite the boot, I saw a hand. I turned my light to where our informant last stood. He was gone.

We didn't disturb much of the scene, but it didn't take long for us to learn that the man under the mulch was dead.

Stan called it in, requesting a county crime scene unit and a medical examiner. He arranged for Officer Will Sparks to meet them both on the main road near the Prospect Air Park and guide them into the clearing.

Crime Scene Investigators Jackie Shuman and David Sparks, Will's cousin, set up enough portable lighting to illuminate a nighttime baseball game. They puttered around processing and photographing the crime scene, while Stan and I looked on with interest.

The on-call pathologist, Dr. Morris Rappaport, and his assistant, Earl Ogle, represented the ME's office.

"Wild guess, Mo," I said. "How long's he been dead?"

"I don't mean to be either didactic or pedantic—or facetious, for that matter, but how many homicides have you investigated, Sam, both here and back in New York?" The doctor spoke with a New Jersey accent.

"I don't know—lots."

"As well as I, you know when a body goes into rigor and when it relaxes. You can read lividity, and you have a working nose. How long do you think?"

"Couple of days."

"Ah, a couple of days—bingo, that would be my guess, too. I'll only know more after the autopsy."

I shrugged. "A couple of days it is."

"God bless you, Sam-a-la, you're a credit to your profession. I say that with all sincerity."

"Thanks for the compliment. You've boosted my ego for another three thousand miles. Have you found any bullet holes, knife wounds, bludgeon or ligature marks, tire tracks, blah, blah, blah?"

"You'll plotz when I tell you, boychek, but you know what first comes to mind?"

"How could I possibly know, Morris?"

"Vampires."

* * * *

The doctor stared at me with a smug look. Earl frowned, perhaps wondering if Morris was serious, and Stan shook his head, probably wishing he'd taken a sick day.

"What?" Incredulity oozed from my question.

Morris grinned like Boris Karloff. "You heard me. Look at his forearm. See the two spots? Puncture marks."

I looked. "Son-of-a-bitch."

"My thoughts exactly," the doctor said.

Obviously, a vampire wasn't a viable suspect in our 'unattended death' investigation. So, how else or who else could account for the fang marks?

The crime scene investigators finished their work. Dr. Rappaport and Earl bagged up our John Doe and headed for the UT Forensics Lab. Stanley and I stood there with Sparks and looked at each other.

"The guy had fang marks on his forearm," I said.

"Yeah, I saw them," Stan said.

"You believe in vampires?"

"Us peoples-of-color b'lieves in all sorts o' odd things—vampires, zombies, werewolves, mean-assed white people—you know. Me personally, I b'lieve murders are mos'ly committed by shitheads." Stanley had lapsed into his Ebonics act for our benefit.

"Yeah, me, too. I wonder if it was intentional. I doubt a vampire or even a big bat chewed into his forearm. What does that leave? A snake? Aren't poisonous snakes higher up in the mountains?"

"I'm no woodsman, but that's what I've heard."

"You think he got bitten up on some mountain and someone dragged his ass down here to cover with leaves? Not too logical, is it?"

"Nope."

"Snake handlers," Will Sparks said as he stood by patiently watching his supervisors kick around possibilities.

"Huh?" I said.

"Snake handlers," he repeated. "Sometimes they gets bit, and 'cause snake handlin' ain't legal no more, nobody don't wanna 'fess up."

"You talking about religious-type snake worshipers?"

"No, boss." Will shook his head. "They don't worship no snakes. They jest use them in their church services. Have done fer years."

"We've got snake handlers in Prospect?"

"I suspect so."

Stanley and I looked at each other. He shook his head. I shrugged. Will smiled.

* * * *

Two hours before I sent out a general press release, I called my TV reporter friend, Rachel Williamson, and told her about my new dilemma. I suggested that if she hustled a cameraman to the woods, she could scoop the competition.

She tells me when I say things like that that I sound like Walter Winchell. Rachel was born in 1966. Winchell died in '72. I doubted those two ever met.

Rachel aired the first story about our unidentified body at eleven o'clock that night, three hours after John Deere introduced us to John Doe. The cameraman who arrived less than an hour after she and I talked did what cameramen all over the world do at cold crime scenes—photograph nothing but empty ground.

* * * *

The next morning at breakfast, I asked my wife Katherine, the former academic, "Does UT have a theology department?"

"I don't think so. Would you like more coffee? There's a little extra," she said, standing next to the coffee maker.

"No, thanks. I'm good. Who could teach me about snake handlers?"

"You could try a sociologist. I don't think snake handling fits in with recognized theology." She returned to the table and sat down.

"Do sociologists advertise in the Yellow Pages?" I asked in between a mouthful of cereal and a bite of toast.

"Sure, but there was a big ad in the newspaper yesterday. A spring special. Three pounds of sociology for a dollar."

* * * *

Later that morning, standing in the doorway to my office, I said, "Hey Betts, while we're waiting for the ME's report on the body and Jackie's fingerprint search for an identity, I'm going up to UT and see if Will's idea of snake handlers is worth exploring."

"I'll hold down the fort, darlin'."

"As soon as you get a name on our John Doe, run him every way you can think of—financial info, credit cards, telephone records, motor vehicles—the whole nine yards. If the local missing persons' search comes up negative, call Ralph Oliveri and see if the Feds have anything from out of state."

"Okey dokey," she said.

* * * *

Joseph Prendergast, a professor of sociology with a great personal interest in comparative religions, sat across a desk from me in a small crowded office at the University of Tennessee, Knoxville campus. Books and papers were stacked on every usable surface. The floor handled any overflow.

Dr. Prendergast looked to be in his mid-fifties. Short and paunchy, with thinning white hair, and a white mustache and Van Dyke, he relaxed in a swivel chair with his feet on the edge of the desk, hands behind his head.

"Snake handling is a relatively recent phenomenon—less than fifty years old," he said. "They especially look to the books of Mark and Luke to support their practices. The sixteenth chapter of Mark says, in essence, the believers shall take up serpents and speak in new tongues. Those who believe refer to themselves as serpent handlers. During these services, they do speak in tongues. Fascinating, isn't it?"

"Serpents and tongues—man, am I out of my league."

The professor smiled, swung his feet down and sat upright to continue the lesson.

"This may be a recent take on an old theory," he said, "but these folks are very Old Testament, very conservative. They advocate long hair and long dresses and no makeup for women. The men have short hair and always wear long sleeve shirts. The preachers see themselves as faith healers."

"Do we have any serpent handling churches in this area?"

"There are some other areas of the country where snake handling has sprung up, but Southern Appalachia is the stronghold—Alabama, Georgia, Tennessee, Kentucky, etcetera. It's been outlawed most everywhere, but of course, that doesn't stop those who want to believe and practice." He paused and gave me a knowing smile, implying he had the inside track on these people. "Every so often we hear about someone being bitten…sometimes resulting in death." He raised his eyebrows for a dramatic effect.

I thought he might have practiced his act and performed it more than once before.

"To answer your question, Chief, yes, there are churches in the Smokies where they still use poisonous snakes in their services."

"There are over two hundred churches in Blount County. Give me a hint on how to find those who make *serpents* part of their Sundays."

He grinned knowingly again. "Look for some key words in their names. Words like Rural, Holiness, Pentecostal. In your area, I know of one. It makes use of all those terms, The Prospect Rural Pentecostal Church of His Holiness the Lord Jesus."

"Son-of-a-gun," I said.

* * * *

Coincidentally, that particular church occupied a spot in the sparsely populated valley not more than a mile from the airpark and our new crime scene. I learned that one Reverend Lamar Manus acted as leader of the flock.

I called the office with this new information, and while we waited for an ID on our snakebite victim, Bettye ran a pedigree on the Reverend Manus. When I returned to Prospect, she had the information waiting for me.

For a man of God, Lamar experienced more than a few conflicts with the law. In 1998, at age thirty-five, detectives from Perry County, Kentucky arrested him for a grand larceny stemming from misappropriation of church funds. The prosecution failed to prove its case, so when set free, Lamar left Kentucky and emigrated to East Tennessee where he stayed a busy man.

More recently, he scored two arrests and one conviction for passing bad checks. A charge of statutory rape, which ended with the parents and young victim failing to pursue prosecution, highlighted his record.

Most recently, a state trooper charged Lamar Manus for an attempted assault with a deadly weapon when he used a twelve-gauge to scare off a repo-man who intended to boost the Lincoln Town Car Lamar had problems paying for.

Manus seemed like one of those holy rollers who lived by his own set of rules and led his followers by some strange charismatic quality rather than by example or with intellect.

By mid-afternoon, Mo Rappaport called in a preliminary report. Our John Doe died of cardiac arrest brought on by venom poisoning, the likely suspect being a timber rattler.

Jackie Shuman had good luck in getting a quick match on the corpse's fingerprints. Thirty-six-year-old Roscoe Stinnett was printed when he entered the U.S. Army where he served for three years as a chaplain's assistant. I began to see some coincidences.

Roscoe and the Army parted company under less than honorable conditions. The general discharge sounded vague, saying only that the Army terminated his commitment 'for the good of the service'.

More locally, Roscoe got nicked by Blount County detectives for running up a mountain of charges on the Visa card of his former girlfriend, Lily Wheelwright. In the end, Roscoe started making restitution, and Lily lost interest in the prosecution.

Roscoe's last address was a single-wide on Munsey Road in Prospect, a lonely stretch of blacktop with more cattle in residence than neighbors.

From the driver's license photo Bettye retrieved, we saw Roscoe as a good-looking man. Later we learned that by using only a moderate amount of his charm and guile, Roscoe had talked the panties off more than a few unsuspecting women.

I drove to visit the Prospect Rural Pentecostal Church of His Holiness the Lord Jesus. On the way, I made a decision for the future—simply call it the Prospect Pentecostal Church.

Bettye promised to track down Lily Wheelwright.

Sitting on a couple acres of farmland, the church occupied a spot surrounded by a large parking area. Around it, I saw neat but sparsely adorned grounds. The church appeared to be either a fairly new or recently refurbished building.

It may have been well maintained, but it didn't have much of an ecclesiastic look about it. The low, one-story building with white vinyl siding and two sets of double front doors looked more like a small factory than a church. On the roof sat a small cupola with a narrow steeple, which bore no cross. There were no windows. A sign naming the church and its pastor hung between the doors.

I noticed a large doublewide modular home sitting some two hundred feet behind the church.

A man dressed in overalls and a flannel shirt used a power-washer to clean the church siding. I walked over from the parking lot.

The man looked my way, turned and continued his task. I stood a few feet behind him waiting. Being ignored isn't something I relish. I stepped up and popped the wire off the spark plug of the washer. The man turned around menacingly with the spray wand at port arms.

He was short and thin, and the expression on his face made him look just a little less intelligent than my spare tire. From his features and countenance, I guessed the first cousins in his family spent too much unsupervised time together.

"Howdy, partner," I said, holding up my badge. "You the Reverend Manus?"

"No, sir, he ain't here."

"My name's Jenkins. I'm with the Prospect Police. You just here for this job? You work here regularly? Who are you?"

"Name's Garland McNab. I'm the handyman for the Reverend Lamar. This here's my church, too." He dropped the spray wand to his side, holding it in his right hand.

"Is Manus here today?"

"No, sir. Not rot now."

I scanned the fields around the church. A killdeer landed in the short grass and walked quickly to her nest. I looked back at Garland McNab.

"Would you mind opening up the church so I could have a look? I've not had a chance to see your place before." I smiled like a prospective parishioner.

"Sorry. I ain't got no keys."

"Kind of strange, isn't it? A handyman with no keys?"

"They's jest got new locks on. I ain't got ta make me no extras yet. Mr. Manus and his wife, Miss Zilpha, they got the only keys rot now."

"When will they be back?"

"Cain't say."

Young McNab was beginning to annoy me.

"Look at a photo for me, Garland. You know this man?"

I showed him the driver's license photo of Roscoe Stinnett. He immediately began shaking his head.

"Don't believe I know him. No, sir."

"Check this one, bud." I showed him one of the death photos taken in the woods.

Garland backed off a step, and his eyes widened.

"That one's more recent," I said.

"He's dead!" He removed his dirty baseball cap and ran a hand through his red hair. "Lord have mercy. Where'd you find him?"

I ignored McNab's question.

"Yes, he is dead. Same man though. He's not so good-looking anymore, is he? Still don't know him? His name's Roscoe Stinnett."

"No, sir. Why'd ya think I know him?"

"He used to live close by. I've been told this is the church he attended." I lied.

"He did?"

"Uh-huh. That's what I heard. And I believe it's true." I gave him a hard stare.

McNab looked taken back, like he'd been caught with his mitts in the cookie jar.

"Well, sir... Yes, sir... Mebbe he did. But he weren't no friend o' mine."

"I wasn't asking if you two hung out together. How many times have you seen this man?"

"Mebbe he's been here. I didn't know him ta talk to, I don't think."

I didn't think Garland McNab was being forthcoming with me.

"You a religious man, Garland? Go to church often?"

"Yes, sir. Ever' Sunday and ever' Wednesday night. Yes, sir."

"You know your ten commandments?"

"Yes, sir."

"Remember the one about bearing false witness?"

He nodded. "Yes, sir."

"Read some annotations on that one, sport. It means, in other words, God's not pleased with those who tell old-fashioned lies. Especially to an officer of the law. I wouldn't be surprised if He didn't do some of that smiting business on those who make a practice of lying—no matter what the reason."

"I don't like ya callin' me a liar, sir."

Who cares what you think, you little troll?

"Just remember one thing, Garland—there are lots of powers out in the world. God's one, and there are others more powerful than ordinary man. You could bring lots of trouble on yourself by running afoul of one of those powers. Understand?"

"No, sir. I don't see whatcha mean."

"Well, you think about it. Study up on it. Know there are things you can't escape. The truth is one of those things."

As I talked my mumbo-jumbo to Garland McNab, a late model black Town Car pulled into the driveway heading toward the house behind the church. The car then backed up and re-traced its path, swung around and parked next to my Ford.

"That there's the Reverend now," McNab said, looking relieved.

"Thanks for your time, Garland. You remember what I said. Start juggling your priorities."

He listened with a look of abject confusion. Perhaps I would have done better speaking in tongues.

I walked toward the couple who stood near the Lincoln and introduced myself.

"Good ta meet you, Chief," the man said. "I'm the Reverend Lamar Manus, and this is my wife Zilpha."

Lamar Manus is difficult to describe. He certainly wasn't handsome, nor was he ugly. He stood as tall as me…six foot, but he was very thin, perhaps only one-hundred-and-forty or -fifty pounds. He had dark hair combed in the style of the 1950s, parted on the left, slicked back on the sides, with a pompadour up front. His narrow sideburns extended to below his earlobes. I characterized him as the kind of thing you'd be compelled to look at—like a gruesome traffic accident.

Zilpha was tall and homely with mousey light-brown hair. Below her chin, she was built like a playmate-of-the-year. She only nodded a hello.

"What brings you out this way, sir?" Manus asked, with a smile that could strip paint off an old barn. "We're pleased ta meet ya."

"I hoped you could help me," I said. "One of your neighbors met with a terrible accident. I've been told he attended services here. If I show you a photo perhaps you'd recognize him."

"We shall try, sir." His smile made me think of a spider waiting for a fly to get stuck in his web.

I showed them the death photo first to get their reaction. Lamar didn't skip a beat. Zilpha immediately became unglued.

"Oh, sweet Jesus. Oh, Lord have mercy!" She covered her face with both hands.

"I'm sorry, ma'am, Reverend. I didn't mean to show you that one. Please forgive me. Here, look at this. The man's name was Roscoe Stinnett. Your friend, Mr. McNab, says he knew him, but they weren't close friends."

"What happened to the poor man?" the Reverend asked.

"The medical examiner's opinion is Roscoe got bitten by a poisonous snake and died of heart failure. We found his body in a wooded area."

Manus shook his head. "Such a shame. People should be more careful when out in nature."

"He didn't die where we found him. Do you know him, by the way?"

"Why yes...yes we do. Mr. Stinnett did attend church with us. He was a pleasant enough man, helped us on occasion with social events and so forth. We haven't seen him in, what is it, Zilpha, more than a month now?"

Zilpha looked like she just witnessed the collapse of the Brooklyn Bridge at rush hour. She opened her mouth to speak, but no words came out. She cleared her throat and tried again, "Yes, ah…maybe so, Lamar. I'm not sure."

"Do you know if Mr. Stinnett had any relatives in the area?" I asked.

"I don't," Manus said. "You know, Zilpha?"

She lost her voice again, but managed to shake her head. I got the message.

"Well then, it seems my investigation must continue and take me elsewhere," I said. "I'm quite interested in churches, Reverend. I asked Mr. McNab to show me yours, but he said you two have the only keys. Do you think I could have a tour?"

"Ahh, you put me in an awkward position, sir," the Rev said. "Our congregation is not a conventional one. We are more a family than an open meeting place. We have many objects of significance to us alone in the church, things of which, I'm afraid, others lack an understanding. So, you see, I'm sorry, but I must refuse your request. I hope you understand."

"Oh, I think I do, Reverend. I do indeed. Good day to both of you." If I wore a hat, I would have tipped it to Miss Zilpha.

* * * *

Springtime in the Smokies can be exquisite. Dogwoods, azaleas, red bud and assorted wild flowers color the hillsides and flatlands. My springtime provided all that plus a corpse killed by either a rattlesnake or a vampire.

Bettye made a little progress. She learned where to find Lily Wheelwright, but couldn't make contact with her. She'd keep trying.

I wanted to check Roscoe Stinnett's home, but never found his keys. So, I asked Jackie Shuman and David Sparks to meet me there. Our CSIs traveled with equipment to pop any lock and make breaking and entering a breeze.

Before I left the PD, Bettye and I discussed the care and maintenance of pet rattlesnakes.

I doubted the local Pets-R-Us carried Purina Snake Chow. What did a timber rattler eat? Neither of us knew, nor had we previously cared.

The big black snakes that lived in the woods near my home supposedly gobbled up the local rodent population. I wanted Bettye to learn what culinary delights would sustain a really big, poisonous pet snake. Then we needed the name of a local source for said grub.

Who knew how long a snake lived? It couldn't be forever. So how did a serpent handler replenish his supply?

Could you train a snake to bite on command? Previously I didn't know or care about that either. My experience with death by snake came from reading Sherlock Holmes' *Case of the Speckled Band,* and in Vietnam, hearing about the infamous 'two-step' snakes of Southeast Asia.

"You know a few local snake experts?" I asked Bettye.

"I know a few local snakes, but they aren't experts on anythin'."

"Okay, three jobs for you, kiddo. See who knows a lot about snakes. Call the Knoxville Zoo maybe. Learn what snakes eat in captivity. Then where a snake owner buys the food. Finally, see if there's an exotic pet dealer around here. I've got to go and toss a dead man's house."

When I arrived at Roscoe's single-wide, Jackie and David had already popped the tumblers out of the front door knob. They waited for me to enter.

The trailer looked to be about sixty-five-feet long, relatively clean and neat, but with the unmistakable look of a single man's home.

We found only a couple of surprises—twenty-four-hundred dollars cash sitting in a plastic container in the freezer section of his refrigerator and almost four dozen condoms in his bedroom. Roscoe bought lubricated, colored, ribbed, scented and even a few flavored rubbers. Each box sat opened, and a few samples were missing. Roscoe Stinnett may go into the local history books as the unsung stud of Prospect.

When I walked into the bedroom, I noticed two very well done neo-impressionist paintings of erotically posed, beautiful women. It appeared obvious that while the ladies were different, the artist was the same.

Upon close inspection, I found two small and carefully camouflaged initials, RS in the lower right hand corners of the portraits. This interested me for two reasons. One, the probable artist was now a corpse, and two, we found no artist's supplies or equipment in Roscoe's trailer.

A check with the IRS told us Roscoe worked for a carpet cleaning company. A great way to meet women and perhaps test-drive some of those condoms. But not where you needed artistic talent.

We found nothing else remarkable inside the home. Oddly enough, no vehicle was sitting in the driveway either. The Department of Safety listed a 2004 Ford Ranger registered in Roscoe's name. It became another item we needed to locate.

Bettye finished her work, researching snakes. After speaking with the headman in the snake house of the Knoxville Zoo, she learned that a snake owner would feed their pets live mice. *Yuck*. Those poor unfortunates could be purchased from several pet shops in Knoxville.

The Knoxville snake man said my theory of religious serpents living indefinitely was rubbish. Snakes, regardless of their pious associations, could live a long life, but were not immortal.

If you wanted to replace or add to your serpent collection, the closest dealer was an exotic pet shop in Oak Ridge.

Lastly, he expounded on the possible use of timber rattlers or others of their ilk in religious ceremonies. He told Bettye that snakes like any other creatures had personalities. Some were docile, some aggressive, and some just general head-cases or pains-in-the-ass.

When it came to the question of training a snake, he laughed. However, he did say a snake could be manipulated. If you wanted to get your serpent into a more user-friendly mode, you could feed them a few extra mice. The food acted as a soporific. If you wanted a more aggressive and snotty serpent, start with one deficient in the personality department and deprive it of food.

It sounded like a snake's personality was similar to mine. Take away my lunch and I'd cheerfully put six rounds in your ten-ring.

* * * *

That night, after a dinner of farfalle covered with sautéed onions, fresh mushrooms, black olives, cannellini beans and garlic in marinara sauce, a loaf of filone bread, and a bottle of California zinfandel, I called the phone number Bettye found for Lily Wheelwright.

After a brief conversation, I fell head-over-heels in love with Lily's voice. I didn't tell her Roscoe had been murdered, simply that we were investigating him, and her name came up. She preferred to discuss her relationship with Roscoe Stinnett in person.

After more than twenty years of police work, I knew it would be a poor idea to interview Lily or any single female alone. So I asked Kate to put on her detective's disguise, saddle up and accompany me to Lily's place.

We drove to an upscale, semi-detached condo complex in Maryville. I parked, and we walked to Unit 24. Lily Wheelwright answered the door wearing an orange UT sweatshirt and gray, hip-hugger sweat pants. It didn't look like Lilly bothered herself with pesky things like underwear after working hours. She held a footed, bowl-like glass of red wine. Lily was a forty-year-old fox.

Unless I learned nothing in the art appreciation class I took years ago, I felt confident I recognized Lily as the subject in one of those sexy portraits hanging in Roscoe's trailer.

I could have been on the verge of hyperventilation after meeting her, but luckily, I brought Kate along to keep me focused. I took a deep breath and did my best to appear professional and see how Lily took the bad news.

"Hi, I'm Sam Jenkins and this is Kate Wisniewski from Prospect PD." *A wee stretch of the truth perhaps.* "I called earlier."

"Oh, sure. Come in."

Lily led us into the living room of her condo. Kate and I sat on an ecru-colored leather sofa, and Lily parked her shapely backside on a matching chair. She tucked her bare feet under her bottom and held onto her wine glass.

"Would you like something," she asked. "As you can see, I'm having merlot."

"No, thanks," I said. "We just have a few questions."

"What are you looking at Roscoe for now? Is he in trouble again?"

I thought it was time to see how Lily would handle some shocking news.

"We're investigating the death of Roscoe Stinnett."

Her eyes widened. "Oh my God!" she gasped. "Roscoe's dead? What happened?"

Her response looked and sounded genuine. I explained.

Lily shook her head and took a long sip of her merlot. "I can't begin to tell you how well we got along."

She spoke without a hint of Tennessee accent. Lily wore her long dark hair up and pinned behind her head, but several strands on each side hung lose, making her look incredibly sexy. I assumed she knew that and had carefully arranged her hair that way. "We were doing great until he started spending like a drunken sailor—with my Visa card," she said. "Then he started getting sort of, I don't know, distant, I guess."

"How long were you two together?" I asked.

"About a year. Then the credit card thing happened, and he took off. He left me almost eight-thousand in the hole, and he never back. The charges were mostly at ATMs, but some were from stores where he bought things for a woman—and I wasn't that woman. I called the police and reported him so I wouldn't be responsible for the purchases."

"Did you ever learn who Roscoe was seeing when he left you?" I asked.

"Yes and no. I believe she was a married woman. I heard that he became involved with a church somewhere in Prospect. Knowing Roscoe, that was either because he could pinch money from the collection plate or there were lonely women handy."

"So Roscoe had a roving eye?"

Lily nodded and made a face.

"You said yes and no. Your first answer sounded like you based it on his personality. Did you ever get a name or learn something more about the woman?"

"I heard something from a friend who met Roscoe after he left me. I'd guess the woman was a member at the church...the preacher's wife maybe. I think her name was Zelda or Ziva or something like that."

That sounded close enough for government work.

"After he appeared in court and agreed to pay back what I lost in the credit card business, I went to his place and wanted to make up," Lily said. "Boy, was I a fool."

"How so," Kate asked.

"If you ever met Roscoe you'd know he could charm the chrome off a trailer hitch."

She looked at Kate. Kate nodded. Lily nodded again and continued.

What was that about? What did Kate know that I didn't?

"Did you know he was an artist?" Lily asked.

I nodded. "Yes. We found evidence to that effect."

"When I got to Roscoe's place, I saw he had just finished a new painting," she said. "The subject was some woman built like a brick shithouse…excuse my language. I went into a rage. 'You bastard!' I said. 'I gave you everything I had. You took my money. I loved you, and you left me for someone else, you bastard!' I was livid. I told him a few other things I don't want to repeat now, and I left. That was the last time I saw him."

I really wanted to hear what she wouldn't repeat, but before I could speak, Kate asked, "Did you ever find out who the woman in the painting was?"

"Not specifically, no. I think if you find that fundamentalist church, you'll find Roscoe's new girlfriend. Or who knows how many he's had since me? He was a snake. He wasn't a religious man."

Interesting choice of phrases.

"Did he have any relatives in this area?" I asked.

"I didn't know of any. He told me he grew up in Alabama—somewhere near Montgomery—Watonka, Wetumpka—something like that."

"Did you really love Roscoe, Lily?" Kate asked.

She took a sip of wine and looked as if she was getting little misty. "If you ever met him you wouldn't ask."

Kate nodded again. "I'm so sorry."

A wave of jealousy swept over me.

On the ride home, Kate asked, "Did you see the painting she mentioned?"

"Yep."

"Was the woman that good-looking?"

"Yes and no."

"You sound like Lily."

"There were two paintings. One was obviously Lily. And Lily is a good-looking girl, in person and in Roscoe's painting. And Roscoe was a talented artist. The other portrait showed the brick shithouse Lily spoke of, but if that was the preacher's wife—her name is Zilpha, not Zelda or

181

Ziva, then Roscoe decided to be artistically gratuitous with her features. Zilpha is built like a Playboy bunny, but she's not a pretty woman.

"An artist who favorably embellishes what nature did not actually bestow upon his model would probably gain that model's thanks and loyalty."

"Aren't you just so observant and philosophical?"

"I'm a part-time detective. It's what I do."

"Right. Just don't think I'm going to let you join the Detective's Association."

She wrinkled up her nose and made a face. "I wouldn't want to belong to any organization that would have you as a member."

"Thank you, Groucho Jenkins."

She stuck out her tongue like a little kid, but I wouldn't give her the satisfaction of acknowledging her juvenile behavior.

"I wonder how much money he thought he could make at the church or how many girls he could meet?" I asked.

"Most regulars at a church tithe ten percent of their salaries," Kate said. "So there should be lots of cash around. Your sociologist said these people can be pliable. Who knows how many women a con-man can ply?"

"That could represent a nice piece of change. If he created an in with Mrs. Manus, she might give him access to all those holy bucks."

"What do you think the preacher would do if he found out Roscoe and Zilpha were romantically involved and dipping into the church coffers?" Kate asked.

"The Reverend Manus looks like a control freak to me. My guess is he'd sic his attack rattler on Roscoe."

"Can you arrest him for the murder?"

"That won't be so simple."

* * * *

When you have a conspiracy involving a whole cast of characters and there's precious little physical or circumstantial evidence to give you the probable cause you need to make an arrest, you have to find the weakest link in the conspiracy and try to break things loose.

The next morning, I called Joseph Prendergast again for more education on snake handlers.

I sat at my desk and acted like a professor by putting my feet up and getting comfortable.

"Professor," I said, "do you know of something ingrained in the people who attend snake handling ceremonies that could be exploited to get to the bottom of a serious crime committed within their commune?"

"What crime are you talking about?" he asked.

"Probably an intentional murder, at the very least a manslaughter based on a reckless disregard for human life."

"Oh my, that is serious," he said. "Well, if they close ranks and tell you nothing, you're in a pickle. If you can capitalize on what may be an inherent weakness in the types of people prone to ally themselves with a…cult, if you will, any cult, even this group of snake handlers, you may get one of them to speak to you truthfully."

"Can you elaborate on that?" He had piqued my interest.

After a brief moment, he continued. "People who join congregations such as the one you're looking at in Prospect are basically ultra-conservative, evangelical fundamentalists. They're looking for a stern father figure to tell them what to do and what to believe. They're very susceptible to control—they're mentally pliable."

"I remember you using that word before. I'd be interested in plying some truth from them."

"That's possible. I'd venture to say some or even many of them were victims of some form of abuse in their lives. They gravitate to groups like this, often led by very controlling people, because they're familiar with that dynamic, and in an abstract way, they're comfortable with it."

I thought about that for a moment and concluded that I was up against an odd group of suspects.

"Some of these people may well be quite superstitious," the professor continued, "believing in archaic, almost pagan legends. They may fear fairies, ghosts, devils, witches—who knows what. These beliefs have been prevalent in some primitive mountainfolk since the time of the earliest settlers. If you can find someone who is of this frame of mind, they should be extremely pliable, and you may be able to exploit their fears."

The professor used the words *extremely pliable*. My devious mind turned that into *easy to scare*, and once scared, *easy to exploit*.

* * * *

Back at the PD, I began contacting mouse dealers. My second call connected me with a pet shop that wholesaled rodents to laboratories, zoos and snake fanciers.

The owner told me they had a standing order from Lamar Manus. Each month they automatically charged his credit card, and Manus would send someone to pick up a boxful of the poor little creatures.

The shop owner said that so far, each month, Garland McNab would scribble his childlike signature on an invoice for the pack of mice he fetched for Manus.

Do rats congregate in packs and mice in herds? I knew it wasn't a gaggle.

Oak Ridge Exotic Pets, the third shop I called, dealt in serpents— also lizards, turtles, assorted amphibians and reptiles and the ever-popular tropical birds.

From them I learned that over the last three years Lamar Manus had purchased five snakes, the last being a male timber rattler. Because he paid with a personal credit card, they assumed Manus was only a snake collector.

While their facility was subject to inspection, they were under no legal obligation to report the purchase of dangerous pets to any regulatory agency. Obeying local laws concerning the types of critters they chose to domesticate became the responsibility of the customer.

So far, my case against Manus being an illegal snake handler was getting stronger, but I still needed more to prove he killed Roscoe Stinnett.

* * * *

I remembered what Garland McNab told me. He attended church every Sunday and every Wednesday night. At eight o'clock Wednesday night, Stan Rose and I sat across from the Prospect Pentecostal Church in my unmarked car. Purely by accident, I picked a moonless, but pleasant evening, the temperature still above sixty. Stan opened a thermos and poured a cup of steaming liquid.

"Want coffee?" he asked.

"No, thanks. When you get to be my age you won't bring coffee on a stake-out either."

"That bad, huh?"

"Nothing terrible, but wait your turn."

"What are you going to do with this guy?"

"I think you'll enjoy this."

"Why do I always have to be your accomplice when you do these things?"

Stan often whines about my investigative methods.

"If I brought Bettye I'd never be able to concentrate on the case," I said, thinking that would explain everything.

"You're not too old for that, huh?"

Stanley's snide question didn't deserve an answer.

"Look, the doors are opening," I said. "The multitudes are spewing forth with new spiritual vigor. Say Hallelujah."

"You know you're going to hell, don't you? That was felonious blasphemy, man."

"Ha."

It took about ten minutes for the congregation to clear the building and the parking lot. Once the congregants disappeared, Zilpha and Garland stood next to Manus, who checked to see that the doors were locked. That done, the Rev and his wife drove back to their house.

Garland started a battered, yellow Toyota pickup with a white tailgate and a red driver's door, turned out of the parking lot and headed down the road a' piece. We followed the Toyota.

A mile from the church, I flipped on the red and blue grill lights and pulled McNab over. When I stood next to the driver's window, I lit up the cab with my flashlight. Automatically, McNab began gathering his identification. He appeared nervous and fumbled with his wallet, unable to get his fingers to extract his driver's license from a plastic folder.

When Stan flashed his light into the opposite window, Garland jumped six inches and put his right hand over his heart like a frightened squirrel. I tapped on the driver's window. He jumped again, but looked at me. I made a circular motion with my finger, prompting him to roll down the window.

I told him in a quiet but stern voice, "Put your wallet away. You don't need that."

He juggled the wallet before getting it back into his pants pocket, opened the truck door and tried to get out, but forgot to release his seat belt and almost strangled himself. I looked at Stanley who gave me a Cheshire Cat grin.

"Quickly, Garland McNab, we have business tonight," I said, using a theatrical voice.

When he finally got out of the cab, I reached in, took the keys from the ignition and locked the truck.

"Get into the back of that car," I told him, pointing to the Ford.

"What are ya doin' with me?" His voice trembled. Garland was scared—big time.

I didn't answer. I just pointed. He scurried to the car. Stan opened a back door for him. He slid in, and I started driving.

Again, he asked, "Where are ya takin' me?" He began getting panicky; his voice wavered.

"Quiet!" Stanley bellowed, much louder than I'd been speaking.

We bypassed the good cop—bad cop routine and went directly into the bad cop—psycho cop act. Stanley wanted to be bad.

I drove for ten minutes, while we listened to Garland's gibberish about his rights and how we had no reason to take him into custody and how he was a basically good person who never done hurt no-body. Finally, I turned into an 18th century graveyard behind the Prospect Primitive Baptist Church. The earliest marker there showed a date of 1790, the most recent 1865.

I stopped among the tombstones and monuments. A few old trees were scattered around the property. The faint shadows gave it a ghostly atmosphere. We all got out of the car.

"Why've y'all brung me here?" Garland's voice quivered.

I put a hand on his shoulder and scowled. "Quiet, Garland McNab." I then led him next to a five-foot-tall cross with a short, tiered base.

"Do you remember when I told you your God knows when you violate His commandments?" I growled.

He nodded.

"Do you think a person can lie and violate other commandments and his God won't know he's a sinner?"

He shook his head this time.

"Do you think your God is happy now that you've offended Him?"

Another shake of his head. His expression had long passed beyond apprehension. I thought he might wet his pants.

I lowered my head and looked at him through my eyebrows. "You have choices now, Garland McNab, so listen carefully. I know your God is angry with you. If He stays angry, He will abandon you. Do you know what happens when your God abandons you?"

He probably knew, but he forgot and shook his head.

"I'll tell you!" I bellowed, wanting to play my part to the hilt.

I paused for dramatic effect and took a step closer to him. I stood a half-foot taller than McNab and loomed over him, attempting to use every psychological advantage available. Garland seemed unhappy to share my company that night.

"Your soul is here for the taking." I chuckled and smiled malevolently.

He stared at me wide-eyed. "Oh, Lord have mercy!"

"You ask for mercy, Garland McNab," I growled again, "yet you shun your God by lying and committing other sins. Sins don't bother me, Garland. I'd be happy to have your soul."

His eyes widened even more, now the size of Vanilla Moon Pies. "Oh, Lord have mercy! Jesus save me! Y'all are Satan. I knew it."

"No, Garland, no. I'm not Satan. Not the devil." With difficulty, I kept a straight face. "You may look at this big man," I pointed at Stan, "and think he's a black devil, but neither of us are the master—Satan. We are, however, brothers. Do you understand?" I grinned and turned the flashlight on under my chin.

"Oh, sweet Jesus, y'all are the sons o' Satan!"

I saw no reason to contradict that.

"If you lie and blaspheme your God in other ways, you're our kind of guy, Garland. Do you want to give us your soul for all eternity?"

He shook his head violently. "No! Jesus he'p me, no!"

"If you won't join us and you persist in lying to your God, what's left for you?"

He shook his head again, and croaked out, "Purgatory?"

"Perhaps worse! Sit on the ground, Garland McNab. I may have a way for you to save yourself."

He hesitated. "Sit!" I bellowed.

He sat.

I grabbed his arms and pulled him a few feet, putting his back against the tall cross. I cuffed his hands behind him.

"Hey, hey, what are y'all doin'?"

"Quiet, Garland McNab, you'll wake the dead. Do you know what happens when you wake the dead?"

He shook his head, looking frantically between Stan and me.

"If you won't join us willingly, we don't want you." I added a little disgust to my voice. "But that leaves you floundering nowhere. I could leave you here shackled to this stone, and before morning, one of these dead creatures would claim you. Do you want that, Garland? Do you want to spend the night in a graveyard with all these hungry souls?"

"No, sir, no! Please don't leave me here alone!"

"Well, there is a way to save yourself in the eyes of your God. Do you know how?"

This time his head nodded up and down incessantly like a little Bobble Head dog in the back window of a car.

"What, Garland, what?" I said impatiently.

"Oh, I do. I do. I need ta confess my sins and ask the Lord God ta forgive me."

I grinned. "Exactly, Garland," and stretched out the words. "Now, if you want to save your soul, I'll facilitate your confession. I'll ask you questions, and you answer your God. Tell Him what you've done and apologize each time. You understand?"

He nodded frantically.

"Do you worship serpents, Garland McNab?"

"No, no, Lord have mercy. We don't worship no serpents. As Mark said, we take up serpents. We tempt them 'cause we're true believers. We know the Lord will protect us."

"Was Roscoe Stinnett a true believer who handled serpents?"

"He was. Yes, sir, he was. Lord forgive me fer lyin' about that ta ya."

"He forgives you, Garland. Now tell Him more about Roscoe."

"Roscoe, he was a'learnin' tongues and how ta handle snakes from the Reverend Lamar. I watched Lamar teach him the ways."

"Roscoe was killed by a serpent," I said. "Why did that happen to a true believer?"

He sighed before speaking. "Roscoe sinned. He sinned terrible. Then he lied about it. Reverend Lamar tol' me Roscoe committed adultery. He used his evil ways ta trick Miss Zilpha."

Stanley decided to stick in his two cents. "How, Garland? How? Now is not the time to hold anything back!"

I rolled my eyes, and Garland couldn't get his next words out quick enough.

"Yes, sir! Yes, sir! I'm gonna tell ya. The Reverend…he said Roscoe was in league with the devil. Oh, God, jest like you."

Garland must have thought he said the wrong thing. He cringed, pulled his head down to his shoulders and closed his eyes. I let it pass. In a moment, he looked up. I smiled and gestured for him to talk further. He continued.

"Roscoe tricked Miss Zilpha inta his bed. Then the Reverend, he brought Zilpha inta the church one day and asked Roscoe why he took her down the path o' sin, why Roscoe took Zilpha away from him. Roscoe, him bein' in league with Satan, he lied, said he ain't done nuthin' o' the kind."

Stan stood by patiently, shaking his head. He couldn't kid me; I knew he enjoyed every minute of that night.

I looked back at McNab as he continued.

"Then the Reverend says ta Roscoe, 'If'n y'all are innocent, take up this serpent, and God will prove you pure an' good.' Roscoe, he says, 'No, I ain't messin' with no snake.' But the Reverend, he throws that big ol' snake ta Roscoe. He says if Roscoe tol' the truth, the Lord would protect him, but if'n Roscoe lied, the serpent would claim his body…and his soul."

"I guess we can figure Roscoe was a liar, huh?" I asked.

Garland nodded and let his shoulders drop. He looked exhausted.

"And when Manus asked, you took Roscoe to the woods to bury his body under the leaves?"

He nodded again. "Yes, sir."

"Thou shalt not unlawfully dispose of a body!" I cried. "Apologize to God, Garland."

He did.

"You took Roscoe's truck, too, didn't you?"

"Yes, sir."

"Thou shalt not steal—especially motor vehicles. Apologize to God."

He did.

"Before I let you up, Garland Mc Nab, will you put all these confessions in writing and apologize to God again so we have a record of your repentance?"

"Yes, sir."

"Will you show us where you hid Roscoe's truck?"

He agreed, and after un-cuffing him and helping him back into my car, he did. Roscoe's truck contained, among other things, his entire collection of artist's equipment, in boxes designed for travelling. I guessed Roscoe liked to do location work.

For more than an hour, back at the PD, Stan and I helped Garland write his statement.

Using that plus the information we gathered from all the other people we interviewed, I prepared the applications for arrest and search warrants for Lamar Manus and the Prospect Rural Pentecostal Church of His Holiness the Lord Jesus.

Garland would remain a guest of the city of Prospect for the night. I doubted he would get much punishment for his part in the caper, the charges being less than felony weight, and the method I used to extract his confession somewhat unorthodox.

But he could cool his heels for a while in one of our cells, reflect on his evil deeds and plan how to reshape his future.

In the morning, I'd drop him on Chief Assistant District Attorney General Moira Menzies when I went to visit a judge for the warrants.

I poured two cups of coffee and handed one to Stanley. We sat in the two guest chairs in front of my desk.

"You called me a black devil," he said, matter-of-factly.

"Seemed appropriate at the time."

"Where'd you come up with the sons of Satan act?"

"I improvised."

"I heard whattchew said ta him. I'll tell ya again, you gonna burn in Hell—guar-ron-teed. You a bonafide heathen."

"Even though I use my great powers only for good?"

"Uh-huh, guar-ron-teed."

* * * *

On Thursday afternoon, Stanley accompanied me and three other cops to the Manus home. The black Lincoln sat in the driveway. Two men walked around back, one stayed where he could watch the front. Stan and I moseyed up to the front door. I knocked. We waited, and I knocked again.

Through the closed door, Lamar asked, "Who is it? What do you want?"

Not exactly your average greeting. I assumed he knew who we were. I told him anyway.

"This is a house of God," he shouted. "You have no right here."

"Actually, Reverend, I have a warrant to trump that idea. Open the door, or we'll kick it in."

"Go away. This is the House of the Lord, and there is no place for your evil."

I looked at Stanley. "Kick down that door, you big devil."

Before Stan could hit the door, we heard a female voice gasp and yell, "No, Lamar, stop!"

When you're two-hundred-and-thirty-five pounds, one well-placed kick usually does the trick with all but the sturdiest of doors. Stan hit the door and stepped behind the frame to his left. I crouched down on the right side with my gun out as the door swung on its hinges.

Ten feet from us with his back to a sofa, Lamar held Zilpha around the waist. He had a cheap single barrel shotgun in his right hand, held across their bodies.

Stan poked his head around the splintered doorjamb and pointed his Glock at Manus.

"What the hell do you think you're doing, Lamar?" I asked. "Put down that goddamn hillbilly shotgun, and let her go."

"Do not take His name in vain!" he called out, almost chanting.

"Yeah, right. Sorry. What do you think is going to happen here? You think we're going to just leave and let you two continue to dance?"

He gave no answer.

"Put the gun down, and let her go," I said again.

But before he could speak or act, Zilpha bit his hand so hard that the gun discharged taking out a glass fronted china cabinet in the dining area of the great room.

Stan and I were on him in seconds. Stan grabbed Lamar in a headlock until he dropped the gun, and Zilpha latched onto me and began to cry.

Once we had Manus in cuffs and Zilpha calmed down, I called County Animal Control to take custody of the snakes. I suggested that they be given to the Knoxville Zoo and held there in case some perverse judge absolutely needed a couple of serpents in his courtroom during a trial.

* * * *

I called Rachel and told her about the arrest, once again using my Walter Winchell line about scooping the competition. She told me I should be employed by some great metropolitan police department, little Prospect being too tame for the likes of me. She knows how to flatter a retired big city detective lieutenant.

Lamar Manus plead guilty to first-degree manslaughter rather than taking his chances at a trial for depraved-mind murder. He's now serving a fifteen-year sentence in Brushy Mountain State Correctional Facility and acting as the assistant chaplain.

Recently, I learned that Zilpha sold their home and receives a steady income by leasing the church to the congregation. She took some of that cash and bought herself a nose job and other cosmetic surgery performed by a doctor with an office in Blount Memorial Hospital. She and the doctor now see each other socially.

One night I detoured before going home and stopped at Lily Wheelwright's apartment.

"Oh, hello again," she said, answering the door in a long sleeved Henley shirt and blue jeans. The top three buttons of the Henley were open, showing a hint of cleavage. Her bare feet showed below the jeans, and she held the same big goblet as the other night. Lily liked her red wine.

"Hi," I said, "I've got something I thought you'd like to have back." I handed her the portrait which until recently hung in Roscoe Stinnett's bedroom.

She took the framed canvas and looked at it. "Oh God, I think I'm embarrassed."

"No reason to be. It's a beautiful picture."

"'Thank you." She smiled demurely and added, "Oh, hey, would you like to come in? Would you like a drink?"

"No thanks, Detective Wisniewski is buying me dinner tonight."

"Oh, sure. Rain check then?"

"Good night, Lily," I smiled and left.

THE END

About the Author

Wayne Zurl grew up on Long Island and retired after twenty years with the Suffolk County Police Department, one of the largest municipal law enforcement agencies in New York and the nation. For thirteen of those years he served as a section commander, supervising investigators. He is a graduate of SUNY, Empire State College and served on active duty in the US Army during the Vietnam War and later in the reserves. Zurl left New York to live in the foothills of the Great Smoky Mountains of Tennessee with his wife, Barbara.

Zurl has won Eric Hoffer and Indie Book Awards, and was named a finalist for a Montaigne Medal and First Horizon Book Award. He has written seven novels and more than twenty novelettes in the Sam Jenkins mystery series.

Author Links:
Author website: http://www.waynezurlbooks.net
Twitter: http://www.twitter.com/#!/waynezurl
Facebook: http://www.facebook.com/waynezurl

Other books by the author at Melange
From New York to the Smokies
A Leprechaun's Lament
Heroes and Lovers
Pigeon River Blues
A Touch of Morning Calm
A Can of Worms
A New Prospect
Honor Among Thieves

Wayne Zurl

If you enjoyed Murder in Knoxville and Other Sam Jenkins Mysteries and would like a free copy of the award winning A New Prospect, simply go to http://waynezurl.authorreach.com

Please post a review of your favorite Sam Jenkins mysteries on Amazon.com.